Copyright

All r

The characters and events in this book are
fictitious. Any similarity to real persons, living or dead, is
coincidental and not intended by the author.

No part of this book may be reproduced, or stored in a
retrieval system, or transmitted in any form or by any
means, electronic, mechanical, photocopying, recording,
or otherwise, without express written permission of the
Author.

Cover design by: Rob Campbell
Edited by: Katie Handley

Hidden Truths

By L G Campbell

WITH THANKS

There will never be enough thanks to all my family, friends and readers. From the bottom of my heart thank you.

Katie for editing my books, I appreciate your time and effort.

Robyn super PA! Don't ever stop cracking that whip.

Not forgetting my husband for making me this amazing cover. I love you.

Thank you to everyone a million times over thank you.

PROLOGUE

"This way. Now stay in there. Pa won't come looking for you as long as you stay quiet now, okay?" My brother Blake warns.

I nod and tuck my knees into my chest so that Blake can close the cupboard door. Blake holds his finger up to his lips to warn me to be quiet. He's always looking out for me.

"No…please. Jed, baby, it's nothing. He was just helping me with the groceries." We hear Mamma beg. Her trailing voice is followed by the loud sound of Pa slapping her and the thud as she collapses to the floor.

I ball my hands into fists, so tightly that my nails cut into my hands. I watch Blake's face turn to anger. He stands up, pushing the door so it's almost shut but not fully so I'm not covered by the dark.

I'm scared of the dark. The monsters come out when the darkness descends. I've seen them. I've seen exactly what those monsters do under the cover of darkness.

I crawl out of the cupboard to follow Blake. He gets mad at me when I try and help him, but he's my brother and we fight the monsters together.

I hide behind the doorway. Mamma is on the floor with blood coming from her mouth. Pa stands above her and lights his bad cigarettes. Aunt Trudy says they are what turns people into monsters. They smell funny too. I ain't never smoking those.

I spot Blake holding the baseball bat Uncle Max gave us. He said if we ever need to fight monsters that this'll help. Since Blake is my older brother he's is in charge of it for now, but Max said that when I turn eight I can use it.

Pa hasn't noticed Blake yet; his eyes have gone funny from his bad cigarettes. Mamma spots Blake and she shakes her head in warning at him. She always does that. Our Uncle Max taught us that you should never hurt a woman. Hitting women is wrong and if we ever see someone doing it, we kill them. Well he said a different word, but I'm not allowed to say it and Aunt Trudy told him off for telling us. As soon as Aunt Trudy's back was turned Uncle Max leaned in.

"Boys, you look after your mamma. She needs you to have her back. Family always have each others' back. We have yours and I promise you'll be free of your shithead father soon."

He said that two months ago and now every knock at the door, every time the phone rings, there's a little bit of excitement in me. I keep thinking it's Uncle Max coming to save us. I know he will. He's never let us down.

Blake runs at Pa and swings the bat hard across his knees. Pa roars in pain.

"Mother fucker!" He grabs Blake by the throat and squeezes.

"Stop! Let him go!" Mamma screams. She tries to stop Pa but he just shoves her back to the ground.

Blake is fighting to breathe. He drops the bat.

I move as quickly as my legs will take me and grab the bat. I swing with all that I have, aiming for Pa's nuts. Uncle Max taught us that we may be small, but we can take down any man by hitting them in the nuts.

It works. Pa drops Blake to the floor and falls to his knees, holding his crotch. Blake coughs and gasps for air. I go to him and wrap his arm over my shoulder, helping him up. He takes the bat and we turn to help our mamma and make a run for it.

She shakes her head.

"Go babies. Go get your uncle Max." She whispers.

We are both torn. We don't want to leave her but we decide to run and get Uncle Max, at least he can help her. As we run out the door we hear Pa yelling.

"Get back here you little shits. I'm the fuckin' president of the Satan's Outlaws and your father! I demand respect! I will make you fuckin' pay for this!"

We don't stop running until we get to our Uncle and Aunt's place where we're safe for now at least.

We went through another four years of living through that hell after that night. During those four years our mamma had our baby sister Maggie May. Mamma had a plan: we were going to leave and stay with Max and Trudy. Mamma said Pa's time was up now, too many members were fed up of his ways. It was our time to escape and be free.

But life isn't a fairy-tale. In just one day the monster was dead. Pa was finally gone, but so was our mamma. Pa's bad decisions and shady dealings caught up with him and the Satan's Outlaws were nearly wiped out in a war he caused.

Blake and I made a vow that day that we would never be anything like our father. We both refused to become brothers of the Satan's Outlaws. Blake should've been president of the club one day, it was his birthright. He declined.

The Satan's Outlaws is in our blood. We will always stand by them and have their backs, but we will never join. We will never become our father.

CHAPTER ONE

Wes

I sit in my truck watching a few members of the Mexican Cartel. For months I've been watching their dealings, their meetings, I know everything about them. I could even tell you who they're fuckin'.

No one knows that I've been gathering intel. Rip, my cousin and the President of the Satan's Outlaws, asked me directly. I didn't need persuading, after the shit they caused I was more than happy to do it. The Cartel want the Satan's Outlaws' territory. They want their business. They want to rule it all. Like hell are the Satan's Outlaws going to let that happen!

I watch and grip my steering wheel tight as one of the cartel slaps his woman across the face for not doing as he asked. I grit my jaw and take a picture on my phone. I have a nice little album coming along of the assholes I'm going to kill. War is coming and these fuckers will be mine.

Leaving the poor woman behind, they get in their car. I chuck my phone on the seat and follow them. Eventually they pull up outside a florist. I tuck my truck slightly back to keep out of view.

They've been coming here on and off a lot over this past month. At first I thought it was because the Cartel were secretly romantic bastards. I snort with laughter at the thought. I quickly noticed that every time one of them comes out of the shop they dump the flowers in the trash.

They aren't going in there to buy flowers, it's something else, some other reason. A dealer maybe? I write down the name of the florist, Serena's Flowers, to have a look into it. A florist isn't exactly a normal place for the Cartel to be.

I watch them drive off. I don't follow them. I don't want to bring too much attention to myself. I watch the florist, wondering if I should go in. While I'm deciding what I should do a women comes out of the shop.

"Shit." I say, feeling like the wind has been kicked out of me. She is stunning. She has thick long wavy dark brown nearly black hair, olive skin, and sexy curves. She bends down to place some flowers in the bucket display.

"Fuck me." I groan, looking at her perfect heart shaped ass.

I haven't even seen her face yet and she's already caught my attention. No wonder the Cartel keep coming back here.

Something catches her attention and she looks my way.

Big dark brown eyes surrounded by long thick eyelashes, a small perfect nose, and then there's her mouth, her plump bow shaped lips. She is the most beautiful woman I've ever seen.

I'm watching her. I'm captivated by her. She smiles as she greets an elderly man. She hugs him and I immediately feel fuckin' jealous of the old guy. He must say something funny to her because she throws her head back and laughs.

I feel like I've been punched in the gut. I know I have to find out who this woman is. Just by seeing her I know I want her. I have to make her mine.

I've already met my fair share of beautiful women and I have had my chance but I've always been the nice guy. I always saw who they were truly meant to be with.

What is it they say? Nice guys always finish last. Well not this time, I'm not letting anything come between me and her. Every other fucker has had their happily ever after, now I'm taking mine.

My cell rings. I glance down and see it is

Rip. Sighing I pick up the phone.

"Yeah." I answer.

"How is it going? Any progress?" He asks.

I pause and look at the beautiful woman in front of me.

"Nah, nothing new to report." I lie. "How much longer are you wanting me to do this for anyway?" I ask.

"Until I know or have some idea what those mother fuckers are up to. I don't like not knowing. I need to prepare the brothers and arrange back up incase it's needed. I need to make sure the old ladies and kids are safe and protected." Rip grits.

"Alright, jeez, calm down. I get it. I'll continue to keep tabs on them. Christ, someone is a little cranky this morning. What's the matter? Rose giving you blue balls?" I tease.

"Fuck off and don't talk about my old lady like that or I will fuck you up." Rip warns.

"Stop flirting with me! We're cousins you sick fuck." I laugh.

"For fuck sake Wes." Rip laughs.

"Listen, I gotta go. Catch you later."

"Later brother." Rip says as he disconnects.

I keep hold of my phone and tap it on the steering wheel, trying to decide if I should go in. If I had my way I would go in and throw her over my shoulder and take her back to mine and never let her go.

I know how creepy and insane that sounds though. I haven't even spoken to her, for all I know she's a crazy bitch.

Now isn't the time to be going after her. I have enough shit to deal with. I've waited this long to find the right one for me, I can wait a little longer.

CHAPTER TWO

Serena

I unlock the front door and walk into the silent house. I chuck my keys down on the table in the hallway and pick up the huge pile of mail that had gathered by the door. I know I should have come sooner but I just couldn't face it. I couldn't even ask another family member to help because there aren't any; it was just us.

I pick up the photo frame of my mamma, my brother Luca, and me. We're all grinning. Luca is at least two foot taller than me and Mamma and has his arms over both of our shoulders.

I sniff and wipe away the tears that had fallen. I sigh and take a deep breath.

"Come on Serena, you can do this." I say, giving myself a prep talk.

Six months ago I got a knock on my door that completely changed my life.

It was 11:30pm on a Thursday night. I should have known it wasn't going to be anything good. No late night knock on the door is ever good.

I remember opening the door, seeing the police officer, and thinking that Luca had gone and got himself into trouble again.

I couldn't have been more wrong. I wish he had just been in trouble. The words that came out of that officers mouth destroyed my entire world.

"I'm sorry Miss DeRosa, your mother and brother were involved in a fatal car crash. I'm sorry to inform you that they both passed away at the scene."

That was it, in one sentence. Now I have no one. I don't have a family anymore and I never really had any friends. My mamma was always fussy when it came to who I was friends with, she didn't trust any of them. Unless they were Italian they were not allowed round for dinner.

I never felt like I missed out because I had my brother. He was my best friend and my protector. I know he had friends that he didn't tell Mamma about, but it's different for male friendships. They can hang around at the park and go to parties and don't really get judged. I wasn't allowed to the park on my own. I couldn't play dolls with the other girls when I was little or invite them for tea. I only ever made one friend and that was when I was nine. Her name was Aria, an Italian girl whose father was working in Texas on business. She was only here for six months before she had to move again. We had that in common, never being able to have friends. It was an instant bond. We tried to stay in touch but because she kept moving for her father's work it was hard to keep up with her.

I open the windows and air the dusty house. The bank is taking back the house tomorrow and I want to make sure I keep all of the important possessions. Mamma never had a lot of money and anything she got she gave to us. When my father abandoned us he left Luca and I some trust funds. It was enough for me to start my own business. I also got a house. Mamma didn't get anything and she would never accept our offers to help her either. She would argue, stating that the money was for us children to start our lives. She always said that we were her life and so as long as we were happy, she was happy.

I box up my mamma's jewellery and photographs. I look around her room and make sure I have everything. I spot a box tucked away on top of her wardrobe. I grab a chair and climb up to get it.

It's an old shoe box. I blow off the dust and open it. Inside are some theatre ticket stubs, some photographs, a stack of letters and a few other things. I smile, it must be her memory box from when she was younger. I decide to sit and go through the box with a glass of wine when I get back home. Then I'll have more time to go through it all.

After loading up my car with boxes and a few bag of blankets, I walk around the house one last time, my mind reliving all of the memories we made here. Walking to the front door, I take one last look around the small family home I grew up in.

"Bye Mamma, bye Luca. Look after each other up there. I will see you both again one day. Ti amo." I choke. I turn and leave. I lock the door and post the key in the mailbox.

Driving home I can't help but feel incredibly lonely. It is as if saying goodbye to the last part of our family life, our home, made it all final. I can no longer go and sit in Mamma's armchair just to feel like I'm with her. I can no longer sit in our kitchen and remember the amazing smell of Mamma's cooking or watch Luca stealing bites of food or hear Mamma hitting him with her tea towel and yelling at him in Italian.

I sigh. I know I will always have those memories but somehow sitting in the house made them feel more real. Now I'm worried I'll forget some of them. I will miss the connection I felt towards the home I grew up in. I just have to take solace in the fact a new family will move in and make their own memories.

I pull up at home and unload the boxes. As soon as I've put them in the spare room I head to the kitchen and open a bottle of wine. Waiting for me is my Mamma's box. I sit in my snug chair and take a sip of wine before placing it down and opening the lid. I smile as I look at the photos of her: young, beautiful and laughing. She's with a man in most of them, a man I haven't seen before, probably a boyfriend. She only ever told us about our father and that he was the love of her life.

I turn the photo over, there is writing on the back.

Viola, my world. Xx

I smile, definitely a boyfriend!

"Mamma you sneaky girl." I smile.

I look at the young man in the picture. He is handsome with jet black hair and chiselled good looks; he reminds me of my brother Luca.

I take a sip of wine and open the first letter. Each of the letters contain sweet love poems and promise letters signed by 'Luis'. They are all written in English which surprises me. Mamma didn't speak very good English. She said she would only ever speak in her mother tongue, but judging by these letters she understood English very well.

I get to the final two letters.

My Viola, please keep sending me photographs of our beautiful children, in my dark world they are the only light I get to see. To receive your letters, the photographs, they mean everything to me, my love.

One day I shall come for you and we shall run away together, just the four of us. I am a wealthy man. The children shall want for nothing, I can promise them a lifetime of security. There will come a time where I shall no longer keep you hidden, keep us hidden, I will come for you my love.

Your Luis

Xx

I rub my eyes in confusion. His children.

His children! I grab the final letter.

Viola, why do you continue to ignore me? Why do you hurt me so? My wife...I do not love her. It is you I love. I didn't plan on her getting pregnant, it happened. A mistake. A lie I shall forever have to live.

I am not the man you once knew Viola. This dark world has changed me, I have done things, things that would make your blood run cold. I am a monster. So this will be my last letter to you. You were right to ignore me, I deserve the pain and the hurt.

You deserve the world. You deserve everything I cannot give you. I will continue to take care of you and the children financially. I shall always hold you close in my heart. My heart will only ever belong to you.

This is goodbye my love, I will love you always. We can never be us again in this life but maybe in the next life we will meet again.

You will always be my love, my world.

Luis

Xxx

"What the fuck?" I ask to myself.

This man, Luis, is my father?! She told us she had no contact for him, no way of knowing where he was. She said he was no good for us! Everything she told us was a lie.

I gulp the rest of my wine and carry on going through the box. There is one more letter underneath some more photographs with return to sender stamped all over it. It's a letter addressed to Luis from Mamma. It hasn't even been opened. I tear it open, eager to read what she's written.

Luis,

I am sorry I did not write back to you. I was hurt, hurt and betrayed by the thought of you being with another woman. I hate that she gets to hold you, to kiss you. She is allowed to love you while I am not. I have to love you from afar. Why do you hurt me this way? You promised me, you promised me our family would be together. I took care our children and I have waited for you. For ten years I have been waiting. For that day to come when we could be together. I want to hate you, to forget you, but I cannot. I do not care what you have done. You are still my Luis and I will love you no matter what.

I understand your world is dark and evil and I promise to keep our children safe from it. I will always wait for you, one day we will be together. You'll be free from your evil world and we can be together. I will never stop loving you Luis. One day Luis, it will happen. Please don't give up on us.

Your Viola

Xxx

My hands shake. I drop the letter and the box to the floor and pace around my living room, trying to process what I've just read.

I have a father. I have a sibling. I am no longer alone. She knew where he was the entire time! My whole life has been a lie.

I head to the kitchen and pour myself another glass of wine.

"Mamma why didn't you tell us? Why? Why was his world evil?" I sigh.

The name Luis isn't Italian, it sounds Hispanic. Why? Why would they have to keep their love for each other a secret? It makes no sense to me. The worst part is I have no one to ask about this. He could be anyone. All I have are his name and address, which judging by the stamp date are over ten years old.

I flop back down into my chair and hold a picture of Luis and my mamma in my hand.

"Who are you daddy? Huh? Why all the secrets?" I say to the empty room.

Luca and I were always told that our father ran away, that he disowned us. Mamma told us that he didn't want anything to do with us so he left us the house and money and that was all there was to it.

My mamma said he wasn't a good man, he wasn't a man of god, and that was it. She never went into any more detail. We never questioned it because, well, I never wanted to find a man who didn't want me. I didn't want anything to do with him. He left us and that was that.

I don't know if Luca felt the same. He never said any different and now he's dead and will never know the truth. I may never find out the truth.

CHAPTER THREE

Serena

I didn't get a wink of sleep that night; I couldn't stop tossing and turning. When I did finally fall asleep I was plagued with dreams of my mamma and apparent father.

I go about my morning routine, showering and changing ready for my day at my floristry. I was never a morning person, so I don't open my shop until 10am.

I love what I do: the smell of fresh flowers and making beautiful bunches for people who want to cheer someone up or tell them they love them. A lot of the time they're 'I'm sorry' flowers.

I park and open up. I type in the code for the alarm and switch on all of the lights. The bright flowers and strong floral scent greets me. I sigh and put the coffee machine on as I pull out the displays.

Just as I'm about to get another display out,

two men come in and without even looking grab a few random flowers and place them on the counter. I smile and walk over to serve them.

"Would you like to write a card for the flowers?" I ask.

"No." The smaller one answers bluntly.

"A pretty girl like you have a boyfriend to help you do the heavy lifting?" The bigger guy asks with a thick accent.

"No, it's just me." I answer.

These guys have been coming in every week for a while now. They creep me out and make me feel uncomfortable. They ask weird and sometimes personal questions.

"There! All wrapped for you. Is there anything else I can help you with?" I ask, praying that they say no and leave.

"No, that's it." The smaller guy states placing a twenty down on the counter. "Keep the change." Then they turn and leave.

I shudder and wait a moment to make sure they are definitely gone before taking the flowers out for display.

Once outside I bend down to arrange the flowers. I feel the hairs on the back of my neck stand on end like someone is watching me. I turn and look around. I spot Mr Evans walking with his walking stick, slowly hobbling along with a smile on his face.

"Good morning Mr Evans!" I yell as he is pretty deaf.

"Morning my beautiful girl, you married yet?" He asks me the same question every day.

"Nope! Still not found my prince charming!" I yell back smiling.

Mr Evans tuts and shakes his head.

"My girl if I could get down on one knee right now I would propose to you on the spot." He sighs.

I laugh.

"But what would Meredith say?" I ask. Meredith is his lady friend. She basically bosses him about and he moans about her. I think they love each other deep down.

"Ah, she's a pain in my ass!" He yells.

"You don't mean that!" I laugh.

"No I guess not but she does give me a headache though." He shrugs.

I bend down and pluck a fresh white carnation and thread it through the lapel of his blazer.

"There! Now you look smart for Meredith." I state and kiss his cheek.

"Easy there girl! You'll give this old timer a heart attack with those lips!" He huffs and walks off.

"Bye Mr Evans! See you tomorrow." I yell and wave before heading inside.

I pour myself a coffee and pull out the last letter that was returned to Mamma. I type in the address on the computer but nothing comes up. That's strange, maybe it's been demolished. I decide to do an internet search instead to see if maybe I can find some old maps or images or something. A registry site comes up that you have to pay for.

"Huh! That figures." I mutter to myself.

I go out back and grab my purse.

"To find your estranged father you have to have your credit card handy." I mock in my deepest voice. "I hope you're worth it daddy." I say to myself, looking in my purse for my credit card as I walk back to the counter.

"Sounds expensive." A deep voice says, making me jump. I throw my purse up in the air and scream. My heart beats erratically in my chest.

"Shit, I'm sorry. Let me pick that up for you." He says, bending down and picking up my purse while I stand with my hand over my heart, trying to make sure I haven't had a heart attack.

I just stand watching him; I don't say anything. He looks up at me and winks.

"Here." He steps forward and holds out my

purse. I reach out and take it.

"Um, thanks. Sorry, I didn't think anyone was in the shop." I shake my head. "Um what can I get you? Flowers? Plant?" I ask as I place my purse down.

I notice how good looking he is. He has warm brown hair with blonde flecks, stubble across his jaw, and a handsome smile that makes his deep blue eyes almost sparkle with mischief.

He pauses for a moment, thinking thoroughly about his answer.

"Sure, right, I'm in a florist. Of course! Flowers." He smiles. "How about a random bunch? You can make it up for me?" He asks.

"Sure. Any favourite colours or flowers in particular?" I ask.

"No idea. How about you pick your favourites?" He winks.

I nod.

"Very well. So tell me, your girlfriend, is she pretty?" I ask, walking to the roses. Why did I ask that question?! I never ask questions that personal. It's the whole business with Mamma, it's completely thrown me.

"She's not my girlfriend yet. In fact I'm hoping these beautiful flowers will win her over! Yeah, she is fuckin' stunning." He states vehemently.

I nod, too scared at what my mouth will say next to speak. I don't want to embarrass myself further.

"Hhmm hmm. I will make you a beautiful bouquet, so beautiful she won't be able to decline." I say, leaning up and reaching for the white roses.

I carry the bunch of flowers back to the counter and pull out the wrapping, accidentally knocking over the letter.

"Oh sorry. Do you mind picking that up for me?" I say distractedly.

"Sure." He reaches down and picks up the letter. I'm so busy wrapping the flowers that I'm not paying attention to the gentleman.

"Would you like a bow? Would you like to write a card?" I ask, looking up.

He's standing there frowning and staring at the letter. I lean forward and take it from him.

"It's an old letter of my mothers. I found it clearing out some of her things. Love letters mainly. They're romantic." I shrug.

Someone please shut me up! Why can't I seem to talk like a normal person around this guy?

He runs his hand over his face and shakes his head.

"Sorry, what did you ask me?"

"Did you want a bow? And did you want to write a card?" I repeat the question.

"Do you like the bow?" He asks.

"Personally, it's not for me. I prefer a less flashy presentation when it comes to my bouquets, but everyone is different." I smile and shrug.

His eyes drop to my mouth and he smiles and shakes his head.

"Then no bow. I will write a card though." He states.

I hand him a card and a pen and leave him to it while I finish with the flowers. He smiles to himself and places the card in the little envelope and hands it back to me.

I place it perfectly in the flowers and hand them to him.

"That'll be $40 please." I state.

He scans his card and thanks me and turns to leave, stopping just before the door and turning back around.

"What time do you close?" He asks.

"I will shut at 5pm today." I state, confused as to why he asked me that.

He smiles and winks.

"Great, see you again." He says before walking out.

I let out a breath. What a bizarre morning! It's all normally very quiet unless it's a busy time of year like Valentine's Day.

I pick up the letter and get back onto the computer. I search for a while but it's like he doesn't exist. There are no records of him anywhere. The only thing I find is where the address the letter was sent to is and what it's called now. I don't think I'm intrigued enough to go in search of 'daddy' just yet. I like to have all areas covered and see what else I can find out about him first. After all, he said his world was dark and evil. I have to tread carefully.

It remains a quiet day; only a handful of customers come in. It is 4:45pm and I decide to start locking up. I bring all of the displays in and go around switching everything off. I leave and step outside. Whilst I'm locking up I notice a bunch of flowers propped up against the window. Frowning I pick them up; it's the same flowers I made for the guy who came in earlier today. I spin around looking for him but he is nowhere to be seen.

Biting my bottom lip I take out the card, open it, and read what he wrote inside.

Serena, the beautiful woman with the beautiful smile.

As you may have guessed, you are the stunning woman I would love to take out. Say you'll go out with me?

I wrote my number on the back of this card. I will be waiting for your call.

From the hot guy that bought you flowers. (Don't laugh at that!) xx

I laugh to myself and smell the flowers and smile. Should I be creeped out? I mean, he hasn't even told me his name? I guess he has left it up to me to call him. I know one thing, I'm going to need to open a bottle of wine.

I sit and stare at the flowers I placed in a vase, sipping my wine and wondering if I should call him. I pick up the card and look at his number across the back. I grab my phone, deciding I will text him instead. I'm willing to meet him halfway.

Who are you? Serena x

There. It's brief, to the point, and doesn't lead him on in anyway. I hit send and then glug some more wine. My phone vibrates immediately with a text.

Ring, ring.

"Huh?" I say just as my phone starts ringing with an incoming call.

My finger hovers over the answer button.

"What the hell." I shrug and answer it.

"Hello?" I whisper.

"Finally! I didn't think you were going to answer. I thought you were going to leave me hanging! Why are you whispering? You hiding from someone?" He asks in a playful tone.

I clear my throat. "Nope, just me." I answer.

"Good. I was worried for a minute that you had a boyfriend and I was your dirty bit on the side." He teases.

My lips twitch with a smile. "First off, if I was to have a dirty bit on the side I would definitely know his name and a little bit more about him." I point out.

"Wes. You can ask me anything you want angel. I'm an open book." He answers smoothly.

"Wes. Do you have a wife? Children?" I ask. I know he said no girlfriend but from what I've seen, most men have a wife and a girlfriend on the side.

"No wife, no girlfriend, no kids. I wouldn't be talking to you now if I did. I'm a one woman kind of guy. I don't share and I don't expect my woman to share me either." He answers bluntly. My stomach does a little flip and I'm taken aback. I have no idea why those words affect me like they do.

"Okay. Um, what do you do for a living Wes?" I ask.

He pauses for a moment.

"I own a bar with my brother and I also do some private investigation work."

"You're a PI? Like looking into cheating spouses or more serious stuff?" I ask. Maybe he has the resources to help me find my father.

He laughs and the sound of him laughing makes me smile.

"Serious shit angel. I ain't chasing after no deadbeat husband or slutty wife."

Oh, maybe he won't help me look for my father then. He isn't going to want to help me chase down my estranged father if he normally deals with more serious things.

"Angel?"

"Huh? Sorry, lost my train of thought for a moment." I shake my head, snapping myself out of it. "Um, what's your favourite movie and song?" I ask.

"You're really asking me that huh? Okay well movie is probably Leon or maybe Bad Boys. There are a few contenders. Music is anything. I'm in the mood for anything from Led Zeppelin to James Brown." He answers.

"James Brown, really? I never would have

put you down as a James Brown fan." I say honestly.

"Hey! How can you not love the Godfather of Soul?" He says, affronted.

"Sorry! My mistake in judging a book by its cover. So what else do you want to tell me?" I ask.

"Angel, that's enough about me. I want to know about you. My first question is one I can't get my head around. How in the hell are you fuckin' single?"

I laugh and shake my head.

"Damn that's a beautiful sound. Remind me to make you laugh more often." He states.

"Alright smooth talker. I'm single because I don't have time for a boyfriend and also because my mamma only wanted me to marry an Italian man. That narrows down the dating quite a bit when you live in the sticks in Texas, it's not exactly bursting with Italian men." I point out.

"Oh shit, should I be worried that your Mamma isn't going to like me much? I will say this though, the only person to stop me dating you will be you. I won't listen to anyone else." He states.

"Are you always this intense with the girls you chat up? You don't need to worry about my mamma, she passed away just over six months ago." I say, swallowing the lump in my throat. I don't know when that will ever get easier to say.

"Shit angel, I'm sorry." He apologises.

"It's okay. You couldn't have known." I answer. "Anyway! You haven't answered my question. Are you always this intense with the girls you're dating?"

"So we're dating?" I hear the smirk in his voice. "And the answer to your question is no. I'm not like this with anyone else. I haven't dated in a really long time."

I bite my bottom lip and smile. I'm happy that I'm the exception. This whole situation is so surreal.

"Why me?" I ask with a whisper.

"You're shitting me?! Why you? You are the most stunning woman I have ever seen. Oh god and then you smiled and I swear it was like I'd been punched in the gut. You have the face of a fuckin' angel normally, but when you smile I swear you light up the whole fuckin' world. I knew I had to know more about you." He admits.

I'm actually stunned silent. Not once have I ever been told anything like that. Of course my mamma always said I was beautiful but she's biased because I'm her daughter. My brother always used to get protective when boys spoke to me but that's what big brothers do regardless.

"Angel? You've gone quiet on me again."

"Sorry. I...I just haven't had anyone say anything like that to me before. It has thrown me a little." I say honestly.

"Well shit. I'm not sure where you've been hiding because you must have been hiding for no one to make a pass at you before. I am so fuckin' glad I found you. Does this mean you'll let me take you on a date?" He asks.

I sigh and smile into the phone. I place my head in my hand and shake my head.

"Yes." I whisper, wondering if I'm making the right decision.

"No sweeter words have ever been said to me." He states and I can hear the smile in his voice. "I will pick you up from the shop tomorrow at closing." He states before disconnecting.

I pull the phone away from my ear and look at it, checking that he really has hung up on me. He has. I roll my eyes and chuck my phone down. I glug back the last bit of wine and jig my leg up and down anxiously. What do I wear? I'm going to have to take a change of clothes to the shop with me tomorrow.

I jump up from my chair and go to my wardrobe to search. I hope I can find the perfect outfit.

CHAPTER FOUR

Wes

I disconnect the call without saying goodbye. I had to get off of the phone because I was afraid of what I might say to her. I'd only end up scaring her off if I voiced what she does to me, if I told her all of the things I want to do to her. She'd run for the hills. She has me all tied up in knots. One fuckin' day and she has me completely.

I look at my laptop screen. I had searched the address and name on the envelope earlier. I knew as soon as I saw it but I hoped I was wrong. I wasn't. If what she said is true, her father is Luis, the deceased head of the Mexican Cartel. His son Jesús runs the Cartel now. This is one big fuckin' mess. I can't tell her what I know, I shouldn't even be asking her out.

If what she says is true, she is innocent in all of this and has no idea what she is getting herself into. I just need to convince Rip and the Satan's. Dating the Cartel boss' daughter, well, they ain't gonna like it one bit.

I pour myself a whisky and neck it back. The Cartel visiting her can only mean one thing: the Cartel know who she is. It's either that or she's lying to me.

My cell rings and I see Rip's caller ID.

"Yeah." I answer.

"Update?" Rip asks, getting straight to the point.

"Nothing new to report." I lie. "I followed them today but they were just running errands. Nothing out of the ordinary. Still no sign of Jesús."

"Shit. Okay. I don't like that we don't know where that fucker is. He's in hiding and planning something, I can feel it in my gut. I don't like being unprepared, I want to know all there is to know, I want to know everything. You need me to bring in a brother to help you out?" Rip asks.

"No!" I say abruptly. "No, that'll give me up. At the moment I'm a nobody. You send in one of the brothers they will spot their kutte or recognise their face. We can't risk that."

Rip pauses on the phone and I know that he's wondering why I snapped. That's the only problem, Rip is my cousin and he knows everything there is to know about me. I will have to tell him eventually, but only when I have enough proof that Serena has no clue who Jesús is.

"Wes." Rip growls down the phone.

"It's not to do with this, okay?" I argue back.

"A woman?" He asks.

"Yeah." Is all I give him.

"Fuck. I will keep my mouth shut. Be careful brother. When you're ready, bring her to a cookout." Rip invites.

"Sure thing, will do." I answer, not actually planning on bringing her to a cookout.

"I gotta go." I lie again.

"Wes, before you go, Blake and the women are all starting to worry about you. I've tried playing it down. They don't know about the job you're doing. Just do me a favour and check in with them. You're all good, right?" Rip asks.

"Yeah I will, and yeah I'm good. You all have your own lives going on, I'm just trying to live mine." I answer.

"Yeah, well, just don't forget your family. We've always got your back." Rip says before disconnecting.

I stare out of my window. My family may not be so willing to have my back when they eventually find out who I'm dating. I chuck my phone down on my desk and let out a long breath, wondering if I'm actually going insane. I'm putting everything on the line for a woman I haven't even kissed.

My phone pings with an incoming message. I pick it up, read it, and smile.

Goodnight Wes. Until tomorrow. S x

Yeah, she's worth it.

I type goodnight back, wishing I were in bed with her right now.

****

The next day I'm doing the same thing, just following Jesús' men around. They don't go to the florist today which I'm thankful for. I'm not sure I could've stayed away if they did.

They pull up to a huge gated house. I notice the cameras out front are aimed out onto the street. The house is set far enough back from the road that I can't see in from where I'm parked. There are high walls and high trees surrounding the walls. It's completely secluded. Jackpot. No one local could afford to live in a house like this unless it was the fuckin' mayor, or a celebrity. To have a place like this you have to have some serious dollars in the bank or, in the Mexican Cartel's case, money in guns and drugs. This has to be where Jesús is hiding. I make note of the address and drive off, not wanting to bring attention to myself.

I pick up my phone and call Rip. He's going to want to know about this.

He answers just before I'm about to hang up.

"Wait a sec." He grits through his teeth. I hear him go to leave wherever he is to speak in private.

"Where the hell are you going?" I hear Rose, his old lady, ask him.

"Club business." He answers.

"Club business, is that really important when your wife is sucking your dick?" I hear Rose fume.

Oh shit! He's in trouble. I laugh to myself.

"Sweetheart, I will be really fuckin' quick. Trust me." Rip promises.

"Too late biker boy, the moment has passed. You clearly have more important club business to attend to." Rose huffs.

"Fuck sake, this better be good." Rip growls down the phone.

I laugh.

"Reckon you're in for some blue balls there brother."

"Don't I fuckin' know it. Now tell me

what's so important that it has interrupted my dick being sucked and put me in the doghouse." He sighs.

"I think we've got him. They went to a different location today, a huge fancy as fuck house with high walls, locked gate, cameras pointing out onto the road. It has to be where he's hiding." I point out.

"Fuck me." Rip states.

"Nope! Not today biker boy!" Rose yells in response.

I burst out laughing. She loves busting his balls.

"As much as this phone call is gonna cost me some serious grovelling with my old lady, it may just be worth it. Is there anywhere you can park up unnoticed and keep watch on the house?" He asks.

"Not that I noticed. I will do a drive by tomorrow and scope the place out. There's nothing else there though. My truck being randomly parked up would definitely cause suspicion." I point out. "Let me scope the place out. I'll look at maps of the surrounding area, there has to be a way."

"Got it. Good. I will leave it to you. Check in tomorrow, preferably when I'm not busy with the wife." He laughs.

"Gottcha, speak later." I disconnect.

Laughing I shake my head. My cousin has really settled down with his wife Rose, who clearly has the balls in the relationship. The banter back and forth between them is off the charts. He definitely met his match with her. She has managed to do what no other woman could do, what all the other women wanted to do, be the old lady to Rip, the President of Satan's Outlaws.

I look at the time and head back to shower and change to take Serena out. I feel like a sixteen year old kid again.

"Fuck." I say to myself. I've not taken a woman on a date in a really long time. I hope I don't fuck it up.

I need to get a grip, it's just a date. It's not like I'm going to propose to her on the first date. I'm being such a pussy! The guys would give me shit for this.

On the drive over to pick her up I decide to drive past the house I believe Jesús is hiding in. As I pass I notice cars lining the expensive drive behind the gate.

Whether or not Jesús is there, the amount of cars that are parked up there isn't a good sign. They're starting to have meetings. They are starting to make arrangements. The sooner I can find somewhere to watch over the place, the better.

CHAPTER FIVE

Serena

I locked up the shop twenty minutes early just so I could change and get ready for my date with Wes.

My stomach is a swarm of butterflies. I bet Mamma is turning in her grave at the thought of me going out with an American boy and not an Italian boy like she always wanted me to.

I pull out my clothes: a simple coral tea dress that comes to my mid-thighs, it scoops low across my breast and has little buttons all the way down the front. I'm wearing my cowboy ankle boots because I didn't bring a change of shoes. I leave my necklaces and bangles on and spritz some perfume. I have a look in my little compact mirror and run my fingers through my hair.

"That'll have to do." I say to myself. Just as I'm putting my clothes into my bag there's the knock at the front of the shop.

"Oh holy crap. Here goes." I whisper to myself, trying to control my nerves.

I walk to the door and see Wes standing there with his hands in his pockets. When he sees me approaching the door he smiles that handsome cheeky smile of his.

I swing open the door.

"Hey, come in a second while I grab my bag and set the alarm." I say as I turn on my heel.

I don't make it very far because Wes grabs me by my elbow and pulls me back to him. Stunned, I hold my breath. His eyes sweep my face before bringing his mouth down onto mine. I freeze, unsure at first, but then with the feel of his lips on mine I start to kiss him back. He lets out a throaty moan and his hands grip my waist tight. He pulls away slightly and leans his forehead on mine.

"Shit. I'm sorry Serena." He apologises.

I frown in confusion.

"You're sorry for kissing me?" I ask.

"Yes, no. Fuck! I knew I would screw it up." He says gripping his hair.

"I'm sorry I just kissed you like that. It's just…seeing you look so unbelievably stunning. Oh god and then you hit me with your smile and all rational thoughts went out of my head and I just had to kiss you. I don't regret kissing you, I just regret doing it the way I did it." He explains.

I laugh and shake my head. "Um, well, here's the thing." I pause and try to hide the blush from my cheeks. "I don't regret you kissing me at all." I smile and bite my lip.

Wes groans and looks to the ceiling. "Fuck me."

My stomach does a little flip and my palms become sweaty. I push away and walk off to grab my bag.

"Come on then, where are you taking me?" I ask smiling.

Wes frowns for a moment in confusion over my switch in demeanour but soon smiles and takes my hand, leading me to his truck. I breathe a sigh of relief that I dodged that bullet. Don't think a first date would be the best time to discuss with him my non-existent sexual history. Who wants to date a twenty-five year old virgin? No one.

I was a good girl. I followed my Mamma's wishes. She always told me to only give it away to the person I loved. When you're not allowed to date, you have no real girlfriends to talk to. It's not so easy to lose the 'V' plates, let alone find a boy to date and fall in love with. I've only ever kissed one person other than Wes, and that was my brother's friend when I asked him what it was like to kiss a boy so he kissed me. It was, or so I thought at the time, amazing until my brother walked in on us. That stopped the kiss immediately and then he proceeded to punch the crap out of him.

"Hey, you okay?" Wes asks.

I smile and nod. "Yeah. My mind just wandered off for a moment." I pause. "So where are you taking me?" I ask, distracting him and me from my awkwardness as I lock up.

He smiles and winks. Opening his truck door for me he looks into my eyes.

"Now that's a surprise. You're hungry right?"

He jumps in the driver's seat and raises his eyebrow in question. I nod.

"Yeah. I forgot to bring my lunch with me into work today." I state, rubbing my growling stomach.

His face looks concerned. "You shouldn't go hungry."

"It's fine, really. I wasn't really hungry." I say. Without thinking I place my hand on his for reassurance. Realising what I've done I quickly pull my hand back.

Wes reaches for my hand and places it on his thigh, his hand on top with his thumb stroking in soothing motions. I swear my heart feels like it's about to beat out of my chest. He turns to me and gives me a cheeky wink.

He drives like that the entire time until we pull up at a little restaurant just outside of town. It looks out onto the lake and it's called Joey's steak house. I've heard of it but never been.

Wes helps me out of the truck and holds my hand as we walk up to the door. It's an old house converted into a restaurant. It's all open plan downstairs and the garden and views are stunning.

"Hello, welcome to Joey's! I'm...well tickle my tits till Tuesday! Wes Stone as I live and breathe!" The woman greeting us exclaims.

"Hey Riley." Wes greets back. They hug and then her eyes land on me.

"Oh hell, I am so sorry, I'm Riley. I've known Wes and the boys forever, since kindergarten I think. Anywho! Let's get you a table. Something outside? It's a nice night." She asks while grabbing menus.

"Sure." Wes answers.

"You know I haven't seen any of y'all since Carter came in with that nice English girl. What was her name?" Riley asks.

"Daisy." Wes answers.

"That's it, Daisy. Okay, here we are. Now what would you guys like to drink?" She asks, pulling out my chair for me.

"Could I have a glass of chianti please." I ask.

"Sure. Wes, let me guess, a beer?" She smiles.

Wes nods, his eyes on me.

"Gah! You guys are too cute! Right I'm off to get y'all your drinks." Riley yells before scurrying off.

"She's, um, lively." I say smiling.

"Yeah, she's good though. She'll do anything for anyone." Wes adds.

"So." I breathe.

"So?" Wes throws back.

He reaches over and takes my hand in his, stoking his thumbs back and forth and soothing me.

"You don't need to be nervous around me Serena, ever." Wes reassures.

"I know. I'm sorry, I'm just not used to this." I explain.

"I know you said you don't get much attention but you've been on dates before right?" Wes asks.

I pull my hands away and look down, feeling my cheeks heating with embarrassment.

"Shit! You've never been on a date before."

Wes states. "Serena, look at me." He demands.

Reluctantly I look up at him. His eyes are soft and caring. He leans forward again, taking my hands in his.

"Serena, tell me honestly, have you ever been with a man before?" He asks, his voice low.

My eyes go wide and my cheeks feel like they are on fire.

"Shit. Shit. Shit." Wes grits.

I go to stand, feeling humiliated and just wanting to hide. I don't get far before Wes has me pinned against the wall.

"Angel, look at me." He demands. He takes my chin and lifts my face so I'm looking at him. "I'm not bothered at all that I'm the only guy you've been on a date with. I certainly ain't bothered that you haven't been with another guy before." He states.

"Then why ask me?" I blurt.

He smiles and cups my face with his hands. "Because, angel, I would have gone too fast for you. I would have ruined your first time and I sure as hell should be taking things a lot slower than what they are. Knowing means I won't push you, I will take care of you, I will make sure you are okay with every step we take."

I swallow a lump in my throat and draw in a shuddery breath. I look to his lips and I inch myself forward slowly until our lips barely graze. I close my eyes and move forward, my mouth capturing his. I kiss him. I glide my tongue across his and moan as he deepens the kiss.

"Ahem." Riley coughs next to us.

Wes pulls away slightly and I hide my face in his chest, embarrassed.

"If you guys are that hungry I can try and rush your food." Riley smirks.

We take a seat back at our table and I don't miss the side glances from the other customers in the restaurant.

"Riley, just grab us both the fillet and sides." Wes orders for both of us.

I don't object. I'm hungry and I would rather Riley disappeared right now after I just embarrassed myself like that.

Wes reaches across and picks up my small crucifix necklace.

"Roman Catholic?" Wes asks.

I smile and shrug.

"My mamma was raised Roman Catholic and for the most part she raised us that way too. Strict rules: mass on Sundays, no sex before marriage." I pause, waiting for his reaction.

Wes chokes on his drink. I laugh.

"You playing me angel?" He asks, wiping his

mouth with his napkin.

I shrug. "Maybe a little. Mamma never expected us to be full on Catholics. She said that we should follow the rules and respect god, but she would never interfere or let it decide our lives. We have our own choices to make in life." I state, smiling sadly while remembering her. "But she never let me date and if I did it was only Italian boys." I smirk and roll my eyes.

"She sounds like a strong woman I wouldn't have liked to mess with. She was a mother doing what she thought was best for you. I admire that." Wes states.

I smile. I know he's right. I guess at the moment I feel just a little angry at my mother. She made us follow her rules and be good Catholic children when in reality she was preaching to us while living a lie.

"Angel, let me tell you something, you are lucky that you had a mom that cared, a mom that was able to take care of you the way she did. I didn't get that with my mom. So don't be angry at her for falling in love. She made the choice to raise you and your brother. Your father on the other hand didn't. She may have lied to you but she did it to protect you." Wes points out.

I frown.

"How do you know all that about my father? How do you know about me and my brother?" I ask. I never told him that. I only told him I was searching for my estranged father.

Wes pauses for a moment. He sighs.

"I looked into it for you. I'm sorry, I thought you knew." He answers.

I sigh and nod. "I did. It's in the letter. Mamma told him, he knew. I was going to ask if it were something that maybe you could look into, maybe track him down? I'm not sure if I want to meet him or anything yet but it would be nice to have the option." I admit.

Wes takes my hand and kisses my palm. "I will help in any way I can."

Riley brings out our food and the smell of the sizzling steak has my stomach growling. I don't waste any time diving in.

"Oh lord this steak is amazing." I groan.

Wes laughs.

"It sure is."

The rest of the meal continues with ease and my early anxieties have dispersed. It's turning out to be a great first date. We finish our meal and Wes refuses to let me pay my share.

"Quit complaining. I was raised by my uncle to be a gentleman. That's what I'm doing." He says, taking my hand as we leave the restaurant.

On the drive back he doesn't let go of my hand. First date with Wes and I'm already falling hard. It's the first date I've ever had in my life and I'm falling for the guy. Way to go Serena! Way to take things slow and casual. I practically mounted him in the restaurant! I'm such a goof ball.

Wes pulls up outside the florist where I left my car and turns towards me and leans in close. The air feels electric and I try to control my pounding heart.

Wes gently kisses me, his lips gently caressing mine. I grip the seat, trying to control my hormones and not mount him right here right now. I don't want to scare him off. I definitely don't want him thinking I'm some poor sex deprived nymphomaniac.

"Angel." He whispers across my lips. I love that he calls me that. My eyes flutter open and I look into his hooded blue eyes.

"Fuck you're beautiful." He states, his voice gravelly.

He kisses me briefly before turning and jumping out of the truck and walking around to my side and opening my door. He holds out his hand to me and walks me to my car. I feel like I'm walking on cloud nine.

Stopping at my car Wes tucks my hair behind my ear. He leans in and kisses my forehead.

"Can I see you tomorrow?" Wes asks.

I smile and nod.

"I would like that."

Wes smiles and kisses me briefly before turning and walking away.

"I will call you." He turns around and yells, giving me a wink.

I swear my smile couldn't get any wider. I jump in my car and rest my forehead on the steering wheel and let out a scream.

"Hooooo! Get yourself together Serena." I say taking a deep breath.

I start my car up and head home. The whole drive my mind is consumed by Wes. One date! That's all it has taken. Maybe I'm just that desperate to have love in my life? Maybe that's the only reason I'm falling for Wes so soon. It has to be the only explanation. This is insane, no one feels this way after a first date surely? This is when a girlfriend would be great to talk to, to get some advice. I have no idea what I'm doing or if I'm playing the dating game right. God I'm clueless! Completely clueless.

CHAPTER SIX

Wes

I walk into my house and chuck the keys on the side. Walking straight to the fridge I pull out a beer. I drink it and then sigh, trying to calm myself.

"FUCK!" I yell. I throw my bottle and it crashes against the wall, smashing into tiny pieces and leaving beer running down the wall.

I lean against the counter and try to calm myself down. She doesn't have a clue who her father is or what he was capable of. I sat there and lied to her face. I lied, I said I would help her! I don't want her going anywhere near the fuckin' Cartel. Fuck knows what Jesús would do to her. From what I've researched and seen, that guy is far from fuckin' sane. He is so far off the scale, he's completely unpredictable.

Then there's Rip, Blake, and the Satan's Outlaws; they won't fuckin' be welcoming her with open arms. Me being with her puts the whole operation in jeopardy. It puts mine and the clubs lives in jeopardy. I know I should walk away, I should just leave her to get on with her life, but I can't. There's this pull to her that is drawing me in. One date with her and I know she is it for me.

She's like a beacon, and I'm a moth to a damn flame. Now I've tasted her, kissed those perfect soft lips, I know there is no way I can walk away from her.

My phone rings and I see it's my brother Blake. I pick up the phone and answer.

"Hey man, what's up?" I say with fake enthusiasm.

"Hey man, just checking in. We haven't seen you in a while and I, well, Lily and I were wondering how you were? Just wanted to tell you to stop by soon before the baby arrives." Blake states.

"Yeah, I will. I've just been busy working. I've not had much time for anything." I answer. "Lily doing okay though?" I ask.

"She's...umm...doing alright. Counting the days..."

"I'm not alright! Is that Wes? If it is, tell him to get his backside over here. I've forgotten what he looks like." Lily shouts out.

"You hear that?" Blake asks smirking.

"Yeah. I hear her. Listen I gotta go. I will be over soon, okay." I say before disconnecting.

If I want to have a relationship with Serena I'm going to have to separate myself from the Satan's Outlaws and my family. It's the only way the Mexican Cartel won't know who I am. It will also keep Serena and my family safe. It's the only way I can see how to do it. The Cartel are sniffing around Serena and I need to find out why. I need to know what their plan is.

I pick up my phone and drop Serena a text.

Will bring you lunch at the shop tomorrow. W x

I click send and I don't even get a chance to put my phone down before it vibrates with an incoming message.

Okay. Thank you for a wonderful first date. S x

I smile to myself.

I fire up my computer and pull up the file I have on the cartel. I scroll through each member, all except Jesús. All I have on him is word of mouth, and even then no one speaks freely about him in fear of being exposed as a snitch. Everyone who has spoken out in the past has ended up dead, hanging from bridges or shot dead in their cars. Thankfully that hasn't happened since they moved to our territory but back on their home turf they are feared even by the police and government.

When the Satan's Outlaws had their deal with him he always played his cards very close to his chest. There isn't even a birth certificate for him. He has no records, we don't even have proof that he exists. He has zero record, no trace. He exists but can move freely and do whatever he pleases with zero consequences. The unknown is what we should all fear. We are always treading carefully. I hate the unknown, it's why I do what I do. I have to uncover the truth and find out what the fuck Jesús is up to.

"Why are you so interested in Serena?" I ask my empty office.

It's not like Luis is on her birth certificate. She has no legal right to his money since most of it is illegal anyway. She's an inconvenience at most but a white lie or even pleading ignorance would see her go away. Why sniff her out? Why check in on her every damn day? It makes no sense at all.

Frustrated I turn off the computer and head to bed. Serena is constantly on my mind. The woman is under my skin. It's only been a matter of days since I saw her and now she is all I can think about.

I am well and truly fucked.

****

The next morning I go to where I think Jesús is hiding. I drive by twice within the hour so as not to cause suspicion. I notice a house which backs onto the property is up for rent. I quickly ring the number and ask for a viewing within the hour.

I wait outside of the property for the realtor. I see her pull up behind me moments later. I jump out my truck and I notice how her eyes do an appreciative sweep of my body. Sorry darlin', you ain't getting anywhere with me today. Before Serena I may have fucked her. She's an attractive woman but there is only one woman I'm interested in right now and it sure as shit isn't her.

"So as you can see Mr…" She pauses, waiting for my response.

"Smith." I say, walking past her to look out of the window.

"Err…right. As you can see Mr Smith, the property offers space and modern living at a very reasonable price. The area is quiet and is a close commute to the city and neighbouring towns." She rambles on.

I walk around, looking out of various windows. I walk into what I assume is the master bedroom which has a balcony. From the balcony I can see through a gap in the trees into the Mexican Cartel's property.

"I will take it." I interrupt her sales pitch.

"Oh wonderful Mr Smith! If you could fill out these forms and provide a deposit and a month rent in advance. Oh, and I will need to see some form of ID." She smiles and holds out the forms for me.

I reach into my back pocket and hand her an envelope. She frowns in confusion.

"There is six months of rent there including the deposit. Plus extra for yourself. All in cash, no forms, no ID." I put it too her.

"I...err...um." She pauses.

"Falsify the documents. Do whatever you have to do to get it past your boss." I state.

She nods and opens up the envelope. She bites her lip seeing that amount of money in cash.

"Err, how much..."

I interrupt her.

"Two thousand for you." I point out. "Do we have a deal?" I ask.

She nods and smiles. She reaches into her pocket and hands over the key. Thanking her I take it.

"Enjoy your new home Mr Smith." She says before scurrying off.

Smiling I call Rip.

"I have eyes on the property." I state.

"Good. Any updates let me know." Rip says before hanging up.

I spend the morning moving some of my stuff to the new property. I don't bother with a bed, I just bring my recliner chair. I don't plan on sleeping here anyway.

I look at the time; it's midday. I smile and jump in my truck and swing by the sandwich place to pick up some lunch to take over to Serena.

When I pull up outside I notice the Mexican Cartel's car parked out front.

"Shit." I fume. I don't like the fact that she is in there alone with them but I also can't risk them seeing me. I punch the steering wheel and jump out of my truck and walk towards the florist.

Just as I'm crossing the road to enter they come out and walk past me. They don't even look my way, they're too busy talking to each other in Spanish. I can't understand everything that they are saying, only a few words. They are talking too quickly.

Serena looks up when she hears the chime above the door go. As soon as her eyes land on me she smiles and just like that everything is forgotten. I walk towards her, place the bag on the counter, and continue to walk around to her. I cup her face and kiss her. She hesitates at first but as I sweep my tongue across her she melts into me. I moan deep in my throat as she grips my t-shirt, her nails scraping down my stomach.

I break the kiss and keep my eyes closed, leaning my head on hers and trying to control my breathing.

"Angel." I rasp.

"Why do you always stop?" She breathes.

I groan. She is killing me, just her smile makes me lose all self-control.

"Angel, fuck! If I didn't stop I would be fuckin' you on this counter." I admit.

She sucks in a sharp breath and I see the desire in her eyes at what I just said. Torture, pure fuckin' torture.

"Let's feed you." I state, kissing her head. I need to change the subject before what little control I have left snaps. Sighing and rolling her eyes she nods.

I pull out the sandwiches and drinks I bought and place them on the counter.

She takes a bite and moans.

"This is delicious. Where did you get them from?" She asks.

"The sandwich place in the next street." I inform her, surprised that she's never been there before.

"Well it's the best I've ever tasted." She says smiling up at me. A drop of mustard has fallen on her chin. I reach forward and wipe it away with my thumb and then place it in my mouth.

"Hhmm, delicious." I say, watching as she blushes slightly.

She looks away and I decide to change the subject to see if the Cartel have said anything to her.

"I saw a couple of guys leave as I was coming in, are they regular customers?" I ask.

"I suppose they are. They started coming in more recently and buying flowers. At first I thought maybe they were buying them for their sick mother or something but now…now I'm not so sure. I mean how often can the same two guys come in here and buy flowers. I don't see husbands in here that often, not even the husbands with mistresses!" She laughs.

I tense my jaw. She's right, she's not stupid. I need to find out why they are coming here all the time.

"What do they say when they're here?" I ask.

"Sometimes it's really random things like

do I have a boyfriend or questions about my family. It's never normal customer conversations like the weather or have you been anywhere nice. Sometimes they get a little personal and it makes me feel uncomfortable." Serena shrugs.

I don't have a good feeling about this at all. The sooner I can get to the bottom of this, the better.

"From now on I will swing by every day to check in on you and I will follow you home just to make sure you're safe. I don't like that these guys are making you feel uncomfortable and it's not right that they are asking you questions like that." I inform her.

She pauses for a moment just looking up at me, her big dark chocolate eyes searing through to my soul. She leans up on her toes and kisses me softly on the lips.

"Thank you for looking out for me." She whispers.

"For you, I'll do anything." I reply before kissing her.

CHAPTER SEVEN

Serena

I finish clearing up the shop. I can't keep my eyes off of the clock; I'm counting down the minutes until Wes turns up again to escort me home.

The feeling of having someone there to care for me, to look out for me...well, I've missed it. My brother was always the one who looked out for me before. I've been on my own for so long now, looking after myself.

I hear the chime above the door go and see Wes stride in smiling. I bite my bottom lip as my eyes sweep his body appreciatively. He's wearing black distressed jeans and a fitted white t-shirt that shows off his broad chest. I look at the tattoos on his arm, there's one that flows all the way up his arm and I wonder how far it goes.

"Stop looking at me like that angel." He says smiling.

I snap out of my haze. My eyes flick to his. I bite my lip to try and keep myself from smiling and feeling that now all too familiar blush hit my cheeks.

"You ready to go?" He asks.

"Sure." I nod. I grab my bag and walk past Wes to switch off the lights. I am halted in my tracks by Wes grabbing hold of my hand and pulling me back to him, his arms wrapped around me.

He leans in close, his nose grazing mine, his breath across my lips.

"Kiss me." He whispers.

Still feeling a little nervous and unsure of myself I close the distance and kiss him. He lifts me and places me on the counter and deepens the kiss. He trails kisses along my neck. I whimper as I feel his hardness pressed against my centre. He moves his hand down slowly over the swell of my breast. I suck in a sharp breath at the feel of his touch and Wes immediately stops.

"Shit." He pauses, stepping back slightly. "I'm sorry." He apologises.

I worry I've done something wrong. The only things I have to go on are movies. I looked at porn once but I think what I looked at was more of a kink site. I mean, does everyone use gags and nipple clamps? They certainly don't show that in the movies.

"Angel." Wes calls, snapping me out of my thoughts.

"Huh?" I ask.

He smirks and shakes his head at me.

"You go inside your head a lot?"

"My mamma said I was always daydreaming or away with my thoughts." I shrug.

Wes tucks my hair behind my ear and kisses me briefly before lifting me down off of the counter.

"Um, do you want to stay for some dinner?" I ask nervously.

"I'm glad you asked, I was just going to invite myself in." Wes winks.

I laugh and follow him out after setting the alarm.

As I am driving I keep checking my rear view mirror to see Wes following behind me. I smile with excitement and nerves. God, I hope he likes Italian food because it's the only thing I know how to cook.

I pull up onto my driveway and jump out. Walking up to my door and unlocking it I turn and wait for Wes to walk up. I notice him looking all around and checking out the area I live in. I know I'm extremely lucky to live in such a nice part of town, right in the suburbs. It was left to me by my father. Do I call him my father? Or should I say sperm donor? I shake my head to stop myself from falling down that rabbit hole. That is some deep therapy shit that I do not want to start getting into now.

"You live in a nice neighbourhood." Wes compliments, still looking around.

"Yeah it's nice! I'm lucky my…um…father left it to me. The guy I think is my father I mean." I clarify as I walk inside.

I dump my keys on the side with my bag and kick off my heels. I walk into the kitchen and open the fridge.

"What do you want to drink? Beer, wine, juice, coffee?" I say, leaning over with my head in the fridge.

"Just a beer is good." Wes states, leaning in the doorway.

I hand him a beer and pour myself a nice cold glass of pinot. I take a long sip and moan. There's nothing like that first sip of cold wine after a long day at work.

"Um, do you mind if I change into something more comfortable? I don't mean that in a sexy way. I'm not going to come down in a sexy bit of lingerie or anything. I'm just really hot and stuffy and would love nothing more than to put on a pair of shorts and a tank top." I ramble on.

Wes laughs and shakes his head.

"Angel, just go and put whatever the fuck you want on. You don't have to explain your outfit choices to me. You could wear a granny dress and I'd still think you look amazing."

I blush and kiss him on the cheek before running past him and up the stairs.

"I will be two seconds. Make yourself comfortable, put the TV on, whatever you want." I shout over my shoulder.

I run into my room and push the door closed. I make quick work of removing my clothes and walk into the bathroom. I splash cold water over my face and on the back of my neck. I spritz a little perfume and walk back out to grab my white beach shorts with frilly edging and a black tank top. I pile my hair into a messy bun on the top of my head and head back downstairs.

I find Wes standing with the patio doors open looking out onto my yard.

"Ah I see you've found my old lady garden." I say behind him.

He chokes on his laughter.

"I wouldn't go round calling it that." He says as he turns around, the smile falling from his face. His eyes do a slow and lazy sweep of my body.

"Uh, I know, sorry. Too casual right? I should go and change, put something on that isn't so slouchy." I point out, feeling embarrassed.

Wes stops me and pins me to the counter. He runs his nose slowly along my neck to my jaw, inhaling my scent, inhaling my perfume.

"Your perfume is intoxicating." He whispers against my skin. "You are fuckin' intoxicating." He says as he nips my neck.

I gasp. He runs his hand slowly up my thigh and lifts my leg around his waist, the tips of his fingers slowly grazing the swell of my behind. He nips my ear lobe and moves his hips forward.

"Wes." I whisper, feeling his arousal.

"You feel what you do to me angel? You see what seeing you in these little shorts and tank top, hugging every sweet curve, does to me? Seeing your beautiful face free of make-up, my god! You are beautiful, stunning, an absolute fuckin' goddess. So don't ever doubt how you look or worry about what you wear. I meant what I said, there is nothing I wouldn't find you sexy as hell in." He says as he cups my face. His thumbs stroke my cheeks and his deep blue eyes sear into mine, almost pleading with me to listen to him.

I place my hand over his and turn my face to kiss his palm. I smile.

"Okay. A simple 'you look nice' would have done it." I retort, rolling my eyes.

Wes throws his head back and laughs. He leans down and kisses me.

"Show me your old lady garden." He winks as he pulls me out into my back yard.

I laugh and follow him to my garden. I love flowers and plants, I am a florist after all.

"So obviously you know I adore flowers. When I was little my favourite movie and book was the Secret Garden. Have you ever read it or seen the movie?" I ask.

Wes raises an eyebrow at me.

"Fair enough, you don't really scream the secret garden type. Anyway, the story is about a little girl, Mary, who loses her parents in India. She is sent to live with her uncle in England who has this big grey and gloomy stately manor. Anyway, she finds this locked and hidden garden that is all overgrown and dying. It was her aunt's garden who also had sadly died. She and a young boy plant seeds, encourage animals to come, and the garden thrives. Flowers bloom in the most beautiful colours and it brings love, life, and beauty back into their lives and the big dark manor." I sigh. I should watch that movie again soon.

Wes has gone quiet. I turn to him and smile,

feeling embarrassed.

"Sorry I ramble on a bit." I apologise.

"Stop fuckin' apologising for being you. Your garden is incredible, but let's all thank Christ that I don't suffer from allergies." He teases and I slap his arm.

On the days when the florist is shut I spend most of my time tending to my garden. I have pretty much every flower I could have growing out here. I have roses, tulips, lilies, sunflowers, pansies, sweet peas, and many more.

"This is my favourite in my whole garden. When it blooms it's the most beautiful thing you have ever seen." I say, pulling his hand to get him to follow me.

I lead him to my beautiful pink cherry blossom tree. The buds are just coming in and it won't be long until the tree is filled with gorgeous pink flowers.

Wes stands behind me and wraps his arms around my waist.

"Why is this your favourite?" He asks softly.

"Don't laugh at me." I warn.

"I promise." He answers honestly.

"I read 'A Thousand Boy Kisses' and it was one of the most beautiful yet saddest books I've ever read. The blossom tree was a part of the book that just made you…well…it just got you right here." I say whilst placing my hand over my heart. "The whole book was stunning and is a story that'll live with me forever."

"Why would I laugh at that?" He asks sincerely.

"I don't know. A lot of people don't understand how a book can affect you, emotionally I mean. Do you not find it amazing how some words on a page can make a person, laugh, cry, be scared, be angry or even make you fall in love? I think that's powerful. Only a book can hold that kind of power." I shrug.

"A movie can make you feel all of those things too." He points out.

"That's true, movies can, but you're watching the actors portray that emotion, that particular scene. A book is just words on a page and the rest is all down to you. It's down to your mind to create those scenes, to make those words come to life. That's a powerful kind of magic." I sigh.

Wes doesn't say anything, he just places a kiss on my neck and turns me in his arms.

"You are even more incredible than what I thought." He whispers before kissing me softly.

My heart swells and fills with, dare I say it, the L word. I stamp down my feelings. Easy Serena! Just because he's showing you affection and kindness that doesn't mean you can fall for him in the record breaking time of two days!

****

Wes is sitting at the little dining table in the kitchen watching me cook. I can feel the heat of his stare. I hear him groan when I bend down to check the oven. I may have purposefully done it an extra few times just because I enjoyed hearing his reaction.

"Angel, don't think I haven't noticed that you're doing it on purpose." He rasps.

"I have no idea what you're talking about." I smirk as I bend down to look at the bread through the oven door.

"She's gonna fuckin' kill me." I hear Wes mutter.

"What are you cooking? How much longer do I have to endure your beautiful ass torturing me?" He asks.

I smile and bite my lip, looking over my shoulder at him.

"Well it's a traditional Italian summer dish. Oh wait, you like prawns right?" I panic.

"Love them." Wes smirks.

I sigh with relief.

"Okay good. I'm making gamberi alla busara." I smile.

"Say that again." Wes orders, his voice low and gravelly.

"Gamberi alla busara." I repeat.

Wes groans and looks to the ceiling, muttering under his breath.

"Oh don't say you don't like it?" I worry.

Wes laughs.

"Sweet fuckin' christ woman. You speak fluent Italian?" He asks.

"Sort of. I'm a little rusty but yes, pretty much." I shrug.

"Angel, hearing you speak Italian is like winning the damn super bowl."

I smile and shrug. My mamma always spoke in Italian so it's just second nature to me. It's a passionate language but I never saw it as sexy. Then again, why would I when the only people I heard speak it were my family?

"What's the dish in English?" Wes winks.

"It's prawns in a tomato sauce with garlic and herbs. I also made up a salad and home made bread which is cooking in the oven." I answer.

"You make homemade bread every day?" Wes asks.

I shake my head.

"No. I pre-make the dough and store it in

the fridge for a couple of days. Then all I have to do is knead it and proof it. Easy." I smile and shrug.

"I think I've died and gone to heaven." Wes mutters.

Smiling I start to dish up our food. I place it down on the table and refresh our drinks. The whole time I feel Wes watching me, watching my every move, like a predator watching his prey.

I take a seat and find the nerve to look at him. He smiles and winks.

"Looks delicious." He states, his gaze never leaving mine.

"You need to actually look at the food to know that it looks delicious." I quip. Wes' lips twitch.

"I wasn't talking about the food." He pauses, looks down at the food, and then back to me. "The meal looks delicious too." He adds.

I blush, look away, and start eating.

Wes chuckles to himself and tucks into his.

"Angel, this is the best food I've ever tasted." He moans.

I smile, I'm so relieved that he likes it.

"It's my mamma's recipe. Always one of my favourites to have when it's really hot." I say, sucking some sauce off of my thumb.

Wes' eyes drop to my mouth and I see the heat in his eyes. I swallow nervously. Looking away I continue to eat my dinner.

We continue to eat and chat about random things. When we are finished Wes takes the plates and places them in the dishwasher and tidies the kitchen. Every time I offer to do something he orders me to sit and relax. I can't say I don't enjoy having someone do the dishes for me. No one has ever done it for me before and I could really get used to it.

Wes looks at his phone and sighs.

"Sorry angel, I've gotta get going, work."

I feel a wave of disappointment. "Oh, okay." I say, trying to hide the disappointment from my voice.

I walk Wes to the door. He turns and cups my face.

"Thank you for an amazing dinner. I will come by tomorrow to bring you lunch." He says sincerely before leaning in and kissing me.

I'm not sure what comes over me. Maybe it's that I don't want him to go, maybe it's that I want him in more ways than what I've had. I deepen the kiss, pouring everything into it. I gently scrape my nails down his toned stomach, making him groan. His hands move down my back and cup my behind, his fingers grazing under my shorts. I moan until Wes stops and almost jumps away from me like I've scolded him.

"Shit Serena, I'm sorry. I lose all control with you as soon as I see you but it's especially difficult when I touch you." He says, panting and running his fingers through his hair.

"Stop saying sorry. I wanted that, I want it. I may be a virgin but I know what I want." I say as I catch my breath.

Wes groans and rubs his face.

"Angel...fuck! You have no idea how much I want to take you back inside and fuck you but I'm not an asshole. You've waited this long and I'm not about to come in and just take it. I don't want to rush you into something you might regret. It has only been like three days, three incredible days. We are doing this right and that means taking it slow." Wes states.

He leans forward and gives me a quick kiss before turning and leaving, not giving me the chance to respond.

I watch him jump into his truck and drive off before I close the door. I lean against the door and sigh. He's right, I know he's right. I am just so sick of waiting to lose my virginity. I'm twenty-five years old damn it! I should be able to do it with whoever I want. It's my virtue, not his. I wish he would stop being such a gentleman about it and do me already. I snort with laughter at my own thoughts.

I climb into bed and switch on my laptop. I bite my lip and search for porn.

"Wow!" I gasp as my screen fills with a thousand images, incredibly explicit images.

"Where the hell do I start?" I ask myself as I scroll through. I figure I will start with foreplay. I suppose it is good to know how to do these things. I mean they say all men love blow jobs so it seems like a good place to start.

I watch a couple of videos. I grab my notebook and take down some notes. I move on to sex next and again I take notes.

I know I'm probably one of the only people ever to still be a virgin at this age and to never have even watched porn, but we didn't have any internet when I lived at home. We only had basic TV and if we wanted to learn then my mamma took us to the library or we studied at school. As soon as I moved into this place last year I had the internet installed but the last thing I wanted to look at was porn. I just watched movies, shopped, and downloaded thousands of books.

My phone pings with a text.

What are you doing right now? Are you still awake? W x

I smile and bite my lip. Should I tell him I'm

watching porn? Maybe if I do it will prove to him that I'm ready. Maybe then he'll stop treating me like I'm a lady with a damn chastity belt on!

Watching porn. What are you doing? S x

My finger hovers over the send button. I shrug and hit send. All men love porn. Hell, he's probably watching it right now.

My phone rings: it's Wes. I smile and pick up my phone.

"Hello?" I answer, biting my nail to hold in my laughter.

"Angel, are you really watching porn or you teasing me?" He asks.

"I'm really watching porn. I am a virgin after all so I'm doing some research." I answer honestly.

"Fuck my life." Wes groans.

"I didn't realise there were so many different blowjob techniques! It's not just sucking. I can lick, swirl, kiss, some even used their teeth. I don't think I would do because I'd be too concerned about hurting you. There was also deep throating. I'm not sure what my gag reflex is like but I could give it a whirl." I say, fighting the urge to burst out laughing.

"Serena." Wes says, his voice low, warning me.

I can't keep my laughter in anymore.

"I'm sorry, I'm sorry! I'm not lying though, I really have been watching porn and taking notes."

"Why the fuck are you taking notes?" He asks.

"Well because when you finally stop being a 1950s gentleman and decide it's okay to fuck me and take my virtue, I want to have some idea of what to do." I answer bluntly. I say it straight over the phone because I don't have him looking at me with those deep blues eyes. They always seems to make me blush like a schoolgirl and turn my brain to mush. Over the phone I can be relaxed, I can be more confident.

"You have nothing to research. You being you is more than enough for me. Fuck, it's enough for any man. Not that any man will fuckin' get to touch you though because you're mine and I don't share what's mine." He growls down the phone. That statement has me more turned on than any of the porn I've just watched.

"Angel?" He says softly.

"Yeah." I whisper back.

"Go to sleep and stop researching. When it comes to us there will be nothing for you to copy or compare it to. When I fuck you, angel, I'm going to make sure you hit heights of pleasure that you've never felt or seen before. When I make you come there will be no room to think of moves or techniques, your whole body will be consumed by the pleasure I give you. I will be the only thing on your mind. The only words to leave those beautiful plump lips will be you screaming my name." He rasps.

It's almost a threatened promise. It's a threat I want him to keep, a threat I need.

"How am I supposed to sleep now?" I ask with a whisper.

He smirks down the phone.

"You'll sleep eventually, and when you do, you'll dream of me."

"Goodnight Wes." I sigh.

"Goodnight Serena." Wes replies before disconnecting.

I switch off my laptop and lay back waiting for sleep to take hold. I wait and wait.

"Good damn it Wes!" I yell frustrated and kick my legs about, throwing a tantrum.

I lay still for what feels like hours, wide awake and full of pent up sexual frustration. I know I could take care of things myself but if his words ring true it won't be enough. Thanks to Wes it will never be enough.

CHAPTER EIGHT

Serena

I go into work tired, groggy, and not in the mood. Even the strong double espresso isn't killing the tiredness today. I set up the shop and put out the flower displays. I'm even more tired as I had to head to the wholesalers early this morning to buy some new stock.

An hour or so passes and I'm slumped behind the counter reading through the local newspaper when the two Mexican guys come in.

"Give me a break." I moan quietly to myself.

I plaster on a fake smile and greet them.

"Hey, another bunch of roses?" I ask as I jump down from my stool.

"Sure." The big guy answers.

I roll my eyes. They must think I'm stupid.

They are here for a reason. They think I don't know that my beautiful flowers get shoved into the trash outside. Maybe they work for a guy who wants to buy my shop and they're casing it out?

I turn back around and notice the other guy peering into my handbag over the counter.

"Hey!" I yell.

The guy stops and immediately turns to face me.

"Don't go snooping in my personal items. Fifty dollars for the flowers." I say, holding out my hand.

He places the fifty in my hand and snatches the flowers.

"See you around Miss De Rosa." He states as they leave.

The hairs stand up on the back of my neck and my heart feels like it's going to beat out of my chest.

I grab my phone and call Wes.

"Hey angel, I will be there in about twenty."

He doesn't get to finish before I interrupt him. "Wes. Those guys were here and they called me by my surname." I say, my voice shaking.

"Okay. Lock the door. I'm on my way." Wes states before disconnecting.

Putting my phone down I run to the door and lock it. I write a sign that says 'closed due to family emergency'.

I sit and wait for Wes to knock. I swear when I look at the clock time has slowed down, each minute seems to be the longest minute of my life.

There's a knock at the door and I jump out of my skin, too busy zoned out and staring at the clock.

I let out a sigh of relief when I see it's Wes. I unlock the door and he barges his way through, taking the key from my hand and locking the door behind me. He walks me back until my back hits the wall. His fingers delicately stroke my cheek.

"Are you okay? Did they touch you? Hurt you?" He asks, his eyes searching my face.

I shake my head.

"No, nothing like that. They just called me by my surname. I've never given away my name before, not even my first name, even if it is on the shop sign. I know they bin my flowers outside, I've seen them in there. Why do they keep coming back in here and how do they know my name? What the fuck is going on?" I ask, exasperated and scared.

Wes leans in and kisses me, taking my

mouth and caressing my lips with his. He slows the kiss and I flutter my eyes open.

"Better?" He asks softly. I nod. "I promise that I will get to the bottom of it. I promise I will keep you safe. Now I need you to close up the shop for a while or let someone else run it. Do you have anyone else?" He asks.

I don't want to put anyone else in danger or let my flowers die. I come up with an idea.

"I will close up, but first can you help me deliver all these flowers?" I ask.

Wes looks around the shop. "All of them?" He looks shocked.

"Yeah or they will just die." I plead.

Wes nods and kisses me.

"Okay, let's load them up. I'm staying at your place until this is sorted." He informs me casually like he's talking about the weather.

"Um Wes, is that necessary?" I ask.

He smiles and turns to me.

"Maybe not necessary for you but for me it is. I need to know you're safe." He says before kissing me briefly. He starts grabbing the buckets of flowers and carrying them outside to his truck.

We load all the flowers into both of our cars. I tell Wes to follow me. We pull up just down the road outside a house. I get out and grab some of the flowers. I knock on the door, waiting patiently. Eventually the door opens and Mr Evans greets me with a surprised face.

"Good afternoon Mr Evans. I'm going to be shut for a little while and I didn't want my flowers going to waste so here are a couple of plant pots for your home and a bunch of flowers that I've put together for you." I say and hold them out for him.

"Oh my beautiful girl, that's kind of you." He smiles.

I know he loves fresh flowers. It's one of the reasons he walks past most days. He loves the fragrant smell the flowers give. I carry them inside and place them down. Before leaving I turn and give him a peck on the cheek.

"Take care Mr Evans, I will see you around." I smile. I wave over my shoulder.

I smile and give Wes a cheeky wink before I jump back in my car. He doesn't smile back, he just stares. His eyes are intense, they burn into me and make me shiver.

Driving a little further I pull into a parking lot and get out. Wes parks next to me and jumps out. He turns and looks at where we are.

"Pines retirement home." He reads aloud.

I smile and start unloading my car.

"Yup. Come on Mr Stone, get unloading. There are around thirty-five residents in this place who are just waiting for us to brighten up their day with my beautiful flowers." I wink and walk off into the home.

I hear Wes following closely behind me, pressing the intercom buzzer to allow us entry.

As we walk in I hear the loud sounds of an old black and white movie being played form the living area.

"Hey Serena! Did we order extra this week?" Caroline the head nurse asks, taking a bunch of flowers from me.

"No, these are on me. I have enough here to put some flowers in every resident's room." I say, pointing to Wes behind me.

"Hmm, he's new." Caroline whispers.

I wink and she laughs.

"Good on you girl." She turns and places a bunch down on their station. "Go on through. All of the residents are having social time and their rooms all have vases in." She gestures.

Wes and I go into each room and Wes waits patiently as I arrange little bunches of flowers. It takes me well over an hour.

I say my goodbyes to Caroline we leave. Wes takes my hand in his as we walk back to our cars. I try to let go of his hand but his grip tightens and he pulls me to him. His other hand comes up and cups my face.

"You're beautiful, do you know that?" He whispers.

I frown in confusion.

"You've mentioned it before." I shrug.

"No, you're exceptionally beautiful. It's everything about you. You are this beautifully wrapped fuckin' stunning present. The more I unwrap the more beauty I find." Wes professes.

Any words I had thought of have died in my throat. My chest feels like it is heavy and swelling with the feelings I'm trying to keep locked down.

Wes leans in close and brushes his lips softly across mine.

"Kiss me." He whispers.

I close the distance, reaching up and running my fingers through his hair. Wes groans and breaks the kiss before leaning his head on mine.

"I've said it before and I will say it again, you're guna fuckin' kill me." He rasps.

I can't help the giggle that escapes my lips.

"Come on, let's go home. I will make us some lunch. I suppose I better feed you before I kill you." I tease.

Wes grunts and gets in his truck. On the

drive back I try to ignore my worries about the men from earlier. Being with Wes is helping; it's like he can erase any worry or fear. He seems to have this power to make me calm, with him around I feel like everything will be okay.

I take in a nervous breath as I pull on my drive.

"You've got this Serena, you're twenty-five." I mutter to myself before getting out of the car. Wes pulls up behind me and follows me inside. Walking straight to the kitchen I start pulling out things to make us a sandwich. Wes comes up behind me and places his hand across my stomach.

"You sure you're okay?" He whispers in my ear.

I nod.

"Yeah I'm good, thanks to you. You settle me." I admit.

He rests his chin on my shoulder and watches me make our lunch. I find it hard to concentrate with him wrapped around me. Having him pressed up against me and being able to smell his cologne is really distracting.

I take a deep breath and try to get some kind of control over my libido but any control I had disappears when his thumb slips under my top and starts stroking my bare skin. I bite my lip to stop a whimper leaving my lips.

I'm slicing the lettuce without paying any attention and I accidentally cut my thumb.

"Ow!" I hiss.

Wes turns me quickly and takes my thumb. Thankfully it's just a tiny cut.

"Wes I'm fine, it's nothing. It's not even bleeding. I've had worse paper..." I lose my words as Wes takes my thumb and sucks it. His tongue sweeps along the cut. I suck in a breath as I watch him. He places a gentle kiss on the cut. His eyes are hooded with desire and his chest is rising and falling as rapidly as mine is.

I've had enough. I feel like I'm going to explode. I need him. I want him now. I take his hand in mine and lead him to the bottom of the stairs. I walk up and Wes stops, making me turn back around.

"It's too soon." He states, his voice rough and gravely.

I let go of his hand and lift my top over my head and throw it on the floor. I grab the waist band of my skirt and slip it slowly down my thighs until it pools at my feet.

I stand in my underwear and hold out my hand to him.

"I want this, I need this. I need you." I plead.

Wes' eyes sweep my body and his jaw tenses. He reaches out and takes my hand. I smile and continue upstairs to my bedroom.

Once we reach my room I turn to him, neither of us saying anything. With shaky hands I grab the hem of his t-shirt and lift it over his head. My eyes take in his body, his well-defined muscled stomach, his broad chest. I run my fingers over every part. His eyes watch my movements intently, his hands gripped in fists at the side of his body.

My hands continue to shake with nerves as I reach for the button on his jeans. He grabs my wrist, stopping me.

"You don't need to do this." He assures me.

I smile and shake my head.

"I want to, I really want to see you." I whisper.

Wes lets go of my wrists and allows me to continue. I unbutton his jeans, revealing that delicious V that ripped guys have. I lick my lips and pull down his jeans and boxers. I lower myself down onto my knees in front of him and stare at his thick hard cock. I slowly move my hand to touch it. I wrap my hand around it and slowly stroke. Wes hisses and his hands are balled up in fists.

"Am I hurting you?" I ask, worried I'm doing it wrong.

Wes shakes his head and wraps his hand

around mine. "No angel. It feels good. Wrap your hand around like this." He says as he tightens his hand around mine and moves our hands together.

"Fuck yeah, like that." He groans. He lets go and I continue. Curious I decide to lean forward and take the tip in my mouth to see what he tastes like. I suck a little and swirl my tongue. Wes moans and grips my hair. I take him deeper and suck harder. I like how he tastes and love being able to make him feel this way. Just as I'm getting into it Wes bends down and picks me up and throws me onto the bed. I gasp as Wes spreads my legs wide and rips my panties clean off.

"Fuck." Wes groans, looking down at me.

I don't have time to reply before his mouth is on me. Circling his tongue he slowly slides his finger inside me, curling it up to hit a spot that almost makes me fly off of the bed.

"Oh fuck Wes!" I cry, feeling so overwhelmed. I can't control it.

"That's it angel, come for me. Let me taste you." Wes groans, continuing his sweet torture with his tongue.

"Oh God Wes! I'm coming! Fuck!" I cry out. I grip his head as my hips buck.

Wes crawls up my body, trailing kisses as he does. He leans down and takes my mouth. His tongue sweeps across mine and I can taste my arousal on him.

"We can stop here, we don't have to continue." Wes says softly.

I cup his face and smile.

"Fuck me Wes Stone." I demand.

Wes crashes his mouth on mine. He positions himself between my legs and I can feel him pressed against my entrance. His hands move slowly and pull the cups of my bra down. He takes my nipple in his mouth and I arch, feeling the need build again. I need more.

He kisses his way up my neck to my mouth and while kissing me he slowly slides himself inside of me. I gasp in pain and Wes freezes.

"You okay?" He asks softly.

The pain eases but only a little. I have my eyes squeezed closed. I nod. Wes starts to move slowly and the pain eases with each stroke.

"Breathe." He rasps. I do as he says and start relaxing a little more.

"Fuck. You're so fuckin' tight." He moans.

I move my hips up to meet his movements. The pain is now just a tender feeling. It's starting to feel good, really good. Wes increases his pace a little and once again I start to feel that familiar build up of pleasure. Wes is still being careful but I need more.

"More." I moan, lifting my hips.

Wes moans as he starts moving harder and faster. My nails scratch down his back as I feel my walls start clamp around. An orgasm like I've never felt before hits.

"Fuck that's it angel!" Wes moans.

"Wes!" I scream.

"Fuck!" Wes growls as he comes.

We lay back, panting. I've never felt an orgasm like that before. It completely overwhelmed my whole body. I run my nails lazily up and down his back. At that moment I know. I know that I am head over heels in love with Wes.

"I love you Wes." I whisper.

Wes lifts his head and looks at me.

"What?" He asks.

"I said I love you." I pause and take a deep breath. "I know it's crazy, it's only been a few days, but I can't explain it. I just know. I think I knew when I first meet you, I just refused to acknowledge it. It's okay, I don't expect it back… I…"

"Shut up a minute." Wes orders sharply. I flinch and go to move but Wes stops me and grabs both of my arms and pins them above my head.

"Wes let me go now!" I fight.

"No. I won't." He pauses. "Because I fuckin' love you too. You flawed me. You completely consume me." He admits.

His confession floors me and I sniff away my tears.

"This." He says as he thrusts his hips forward, making me gasp. "This is perfect, it's right, it's fuckin' incredible. I'm not normally as soft as shit but angel, it's meant to be." Wes groans.

Wes makes love to me again and I fall asleep in his arms, feeling safe, protected, and most of all, loved.

CHAPTER NINE

Wes

I sit out in her back yard, staring up at the night sky. I tried to sleep but the smell of her on me and the feeling of her beautiful body pressed up against mine was too much. I've lied to her. She has no idea that I know so much. She has no idea who her father is or that her fuckin' brother is here.

I rub my temples. I can't keep lying to her, but I can't tell her the truth either. If she knew the truth she might want to go and meet her brother and I don't want to put her in that sort of danger.

On top of it all Rip and Blake have both tried calling. I'm supposed to be watching the Cartel's property but I can't leave her, she needs me. I will not risk anything happening to her.

I scroll through my contacts and hit call.

"Yeah." Rubble answers, half asleep.

"It's Wes. I need you to do me a favour and

no one can know about it. Only Rip." I demand.

I hear him move around.

"Shoot." He says without question. That's the thing with Rubble: he's one of the most loyal and reliable brothers there is. He's always there when you need him.

"Here is the low down: I'm renting a house and it overlooks the Cartel property where I think Jesús is hiding out. I've been watching and following them for a while. Rip hired me. No one else in the club knows, not even Blake. I need to lay low for a while because something has come up. Can you take over and do it for me?" I ask.

"Sure, no problem." He agrees without any hesitation.

I sigh.

"Thanks brother. I will meet you tomorrow and give you the keys and address. You'll need to leave your kutte behind and you'll have to drive my truck. Under no circumstances can you be noticed, especially as a club member." I inform him.

"That's fine, you can ride my bike. You need me to update Rip?" He asks.

"Yeah after I meet you tomorrow. I'm laying low for a while. Probably won't have my phone switched on." I state.

"Okay. You good? Anything I can help

with?" Rubble offers.

"No man, I'm good. I will see you at Sigreene Park at 10am." I say before I disconnect.

I sigh, I'm thankful that Rubble has my back. I switch my phone off and get up to walk back up to bed. When I walk in Serena is fast asleep, laying on her front with her hair swept across the pillow. I climb in beside her and pull her to me. She moans in her sleep.

I place a kiss on top of her head.

"I love you. I just hope you forgive me after all of this shit is over."

The next morning we shower together and have breakfast.

"I have to go out and meet a client and pick up some of my stuff. I should be back by lunch time. You going to be okay while I'm gone?" I ask, pulling her into my arms.

"I live on my own. I'm a big girl and I'm quite capable." She rolls her eyes at me.

"Lock the door behind me when I go, okay?" I demand.

"Yes sir." She sighs.

I take her wrists and hold them firmly behind her back with one hand. I slowly move my hand up her body and over her neck until I'm cupping her jaw. Her eyes are alight with desire.

"Are you going to lock the door behind me?" I say low against her ear.

She nods.

"Good."

I nip her ear lobe which makes her gasp. I move around and whisper across her lips.

"Kiss me angel." She pushes up and takes my mouth, biting my lower lip. I growl and move my hand from her neck to her hair and gently tug, tilting her head back.

"You're playing with fire." I whisper across her lips.

She runs her tongue teasingly along her bottom lip. She's goading me.

"I always did like living dangerously." She breathes.

I crash my mouth on hers. My tongue invades her mouth and she moans deep in her throat. I hastily break the kiss and step back. She grips onto the counter to steady herself. Her chest is rising and falling rapidly. Her beautiful plump lips are swollen from our kiss. Her face is flushed and her eyes are full of desire.

"Fuck, I have to go. I will be back as soon as I can. I will text to let you know when I'll be back because I want you naked and in that bed waiting for me. Lock the door behind me or I will be spanking that delicious peachy ass of yours." I threaten before leaving. If I stood there a second longer I never would have left.

I reach the park and see Rubble standing next to his bike and having a smoke. I jump out and greet him. The door of the truck that's parked on the other side of him opens and out jumps Rip.

"Fuck! Really?" I yell exasperated.

"What did you think? That I was just going to agree to this without actually seeing you?! What the fuck is going on Wes?!" Rip growls angrily.

I grip my hair.

"Fuck! I can't say. You have to just trust me on this, it's complicated. If I tell you everything it puts this person at risk and you. It has to stay like this until I can figure out a way around it." I state.

Rip's lips twitch.

"She hot?" He asks. Rubble grunts.

"Fuck off man." I laugh.

"Yup and you're into her. There's no other reason you'd put yourself on the line like this. She's it for you. Well damn! I look forward to meeting her when this shit show is over." Rip states whilst lighting up a cigarette.

"I ain't bringing her to meet the family. She

doesn't know I work for you. There are a lot of things she doesn't know and it's best that it stays that way for a while. She's safer not knowing." I add.

Rip's ice cold eyes glare at me.

"This is more than some little hiccup isn't it? What's the link Wes? What's the big deal? Why can't you even bring her to meet us, your family? I get laying low if that's what you need to do. I get that you want to look out for her and in doing so you aren't bringing her shit to our doorstep. We have enough to deal with. The only conclusion is that it's bigger than all that, isn't it?" He fumes.

"Keys." I hold out my hand to Rubble with the truck keys and he hands me the keys to his bike.

"Don't fuckin' ignore me Wes!" Rip growls.

I spin around and come toe to toe with Rip.

"This club is nothing but a fuckin' curse on my whole damn life! I lost my mother because of this club and fuck?! What about the Rocke sisters?! What about Patty?!" I yell, pushing his chest.

"Don't fuckin go there brother." Rip threatens.

"What?! What are you gonna do, slit my throat? I'm done helping you out. I am, for once, looking after myself. Leave me the fuck alone." I say as I jump on the bike.

"Wes don't be a dick." Rubble sighs.

I ignore him and speed off. I ride. My blood is boiling. I've always done what's right for them, for the club. Now I'm taking care of myself, of Serena. I'm finally putting myself first for once. I stop by my place, grab some clothes, and head back to her, needing to bury myself in her.

I pull onto her drive and walk up to her door. I test the handle to see if it opens and it does. I walk in and lock the door behind me. I walk straight upstairs to the bedroom to find Serena naked.

"You didn't text." She says all sultry, crawling across the bed towards me.

I chuck down my bag and pull my t-shirt over my head.

"I forgot. You didn't lock the door?" I retort, raising a brow.

"I forgot." She repeats back and then bites her bottom lip.

"Remember what I said would happen if you didn't lock the door?" I ask whilst removing my jeans.

Her eyes jump to my already painfully hard cock and she licks her lips.

"Turn around." I order.

Her eyes come to mine and she bites her lip. She turns around on the bed, kneeling, facing away from me.

I run my hand slowly down her back to her perfect round ass.

"Bend down angel. Keep that perfect ass of yours in the air." I order.

She does as I've asked without question or hesitation. I can see her arousal glistening. I slowly run my finger down her centre and she shudders at my touch. I suck her arousal off of my finger.

"Hhmm, fuck! You taste so sweet." I groan.

"Wes." Serena moans.

"I know. I know what you need and I'm about to give it to you. Just as soon as I've spanked you." I growl, caressing her behind.

With a quick motion I slap my hand down across her perfect ass, leaving a nice pink hand mark. She cries out and bucks. I place my hand on her lower back, steadying her. I slide my finger inside her, making her moan.

"You're enjoying this." I state.

She moans again. I remove my finger and bring my hand down and slap her other cheek this time.

"This is me, angel. I like control. This is just

the beginning for us." I growl.

"Hhmm, yes Wes." She moans.

This time I reach around and circle her clit. Her hips buck and shudder. She's already building to orgasm.

"Wait." I order, removing my hand again.

"Wes!" She yells, frustrated.

I smile. I slide my finger inside of her, making her gasp.

"Yes!" She moans.

I feel her starting to build and yet again I quickly remove my finger.

"Oh my god Wes!" She yells and tries to move. I place my hand between her shoulder blades and push her back down. Without warning I slam into her.

"Fuck!" She cries.

I'm still trying to gain control and her walls are already tightening.

"Fuck. You're so fuckin' tight." I moan.

She moves her hips for friction. I tighten my grip on her hips, stopping her. Serena starts to protest but I start moving. I slam into her over and over and I feel her walls clamp around me.

"Yes fuck! Oh god angel, come for me." I grit.

She comes apart, her whole body shuddering. Unable to hold back my own release I climax buried deep inside of her.

"Fuck." I moan.

We are both panting. I pull her up so her back is flush with my front and kiss her.

"I think I might piss you off more often." She smiles.

I nip her neck and kiss her again.

"I should have taken more care. I forget that you're new to all of this, I shouldn't have just dived right in like that." I apologise.

She rolls her eyes.

"For the hundredth time, I am twenty-five years old. Yes I was a virgin but it wasn't by choice, it just was the way it was. Don't apologise. That was hot and I loved it." She smiles.

I feel her clench her walls around my cock.

I growl.

"Well I guess I need to give the lady what she wants." I tease.

We spent most of the day in bed. She erased the shitty mood I was in and the worries I had at the back of my mind.

CHAPTER TEN

Serena

I lay in Wes' arms after what I can only imagine is classed as a sex marathon. It occurs to me that he's never really spoken about his family. He already knows pretty much all there is to know about me.

"Wes?" I ask and I lean up on my elbow.

"Hhmm." He answers. He strokes my hair behind my ear.

"Tell me about your family." I plead.

Something crosses his face but I can't quite place what it is. He sits up a little.

"Okay. Well I have a brother called Blake." He states.

I roll my eyes.

"Well the whole town knows that. Scratch that, the whole state probably." I point out.

"You know who I am?" He asks.

I sit up this time.

"Wes, you were in the same school as my brother. I noticed all of you. Blake, Rip, Carter." I point out.

"So you know that Rip is my cousin?" He asks eyebrow raised in question.

I nod and gesture for him to continue.

"Well our parents died. My aunt and uncle took care of us. Me, Rip, and Blake are pretty close." He shrugs.

"Oh god I am so sorry. How did they die? Do you know what, don't answer that, I'm sorry. I shouldn't ask questions like that. It's really insensitive of me." I say, trying to backtrack.

"Don't apologise for asking. It doesn't matter. They are both gone and that's all there is to it. That's it, that's my family." Wes shrugs.

I frown in confusion.

"Isn't Rip the president of that outlaw biker club? I bet that gets exciting sometimes. Did you never want to be a part of it? Are they awful? Like real criminals?" I ask, intrigued. I've watch shows and often wondered if they were like them.

"Yeah he is and no I don't." He pauses, clearly deciding if he should tell me more. He sighs and give me more of him.

"The reason my mom died was because of the club. My pa used to be the president. He beat my mom. He was a drunk and a drug user. Yet because he was president no one would do anything. They had to follow the rules set by him. When he died, it was the best and worst day all rolled into one. Losing him was like gaining our freedom but it came at the cost of losing our Mom." He says with emotion in his voice.

I kiss his chest and rest my head on him. I'm not sure what to say.

"The club is different now. Rip takes care of the brothers. It's nothing like when my pa was in charge." He adds.

I lean up and kiss him.

"That's good right? I mean I've heard some stories around town and I'm sure they were mostly just gossip." I shrug.

Wes smiles.

"What have you heard angel?" He asks, threading his fingers through my hair.

"Umm, just that Rip is not to be messed with, that he has murdered people and that the rest of the brothers all carry weapons and have killed." I mutter nervously.

Wes chuckles.

"I can't confirm or deny those rumours angel. I will say this, if someone threatened your mom, did awful things to her, what would you do? What would your brother have done?"

I don't even need to think about my answer.

"Killed them. Hurt them like they hurt her."

Wes nods.

"The Satan's Outlaws aren't the bad guys. They are there to help control and keep these towns safe. Just because I'm not a member that doesn't mean I don't respect the hell out of them. I'm not a member because I won't be told what to do." He smirks.

"So you like to be in charge do you?" I ask, moving and straddling him.

I see the fire light in his eyes as I grab both of his wrists and pin them above his head.

"Jesus! I've created an animal." He smiles.

He moves to kiss me.

"Ah! Uh uh, nope. I'm in charge." I wink.

Wes moves quickly, flipping me over and pinning my arms above my head.

"Didn't you hear what I said? I'm not good at following orders but I'm fuckin' great at giving them." He whispers in my ear, nipping my lobe. "Open those legs wide for me angel, give me that pussy." He orders.

I comply, more than willingly. He proves his point by showing me, yet again, that he is amazing at giving orders. I'm more than happy to obey them.

*****

We spent the next couple of weeks making love in bed, in the shower, in the lounge, and the kitchen. I don't think there is anywhere we haven't christened. I can't wipe the smile off of my face. My life has done a complete one-eighty. I've gone from being a virgin loner to a head over heels in love nymphomaniac. I can't stop thinking back to how desperately alone I was for most of my life, even before my mamma and brother passed away. Now that emptiness is gone, that feeling of something missing is no longer there.

We're laying out in the garden and Wes is laid next to me with his broad chest on display. I can't take my eyes off him.

"Stop perving." He mutters with his eyes still closed.

"How did you know I was even looking at you? For all you know I was looking at my beautiful flowers." I point out.

"I feel the heat of your stare every damn time." He smirks.

I smile, liking that he feels it too. We lay in comfortable silence for a while longer.

"Wes?" I ask.

"Yeah angel." He mumbles back.

"Do you think you better put your phone on? You know, just to check that there are no messages? It has been over two weeks, won't your brother and family be worried where you are?" I ask.

He sighs and leans over. He kisses my head before getting up.

"They won't be worried but I will check in now." He states, walking into the house.

He comes out with his phone and switches it on as he sit back down next to me. His phone starts constantly pinging with messages. Before he can listen to them his phone rings. He answers.

"Yeah, alright. I'm on my way." He kisses me briefly.

"My brother's wife has gone into labour, I have to get to the hospital." He states. He leans over and kisses me again.

"Text me and give them my best." I say.

Wes gives me a tight smile and a nod and then leaves. He always does that when we talk about his family. It feels like he's ashamed of me, like maybe he doesn't want me to meet his family. There is something he hasn't told me, I can sense it.

I sit at my laptop with the letters and the photograph. I'm going through ancestry sites in the hope that I can track him down. The issue I have is that he was born in Mexico and everything is written in Spanish. It's hard to make out. I keep typing in each word into my phone to translate.

I yawn and stretch, looking at the time; it's getting late. I thought Wes would've text by now. I drop him a text to ask how everyone is.

My phone pings.

Bored, tired, and losing patience for this baby. How much longer can it be? I would rather be back there with you.

I smile and type my reply.

I hate to break it to you but labour can take hours, even days. Wishing you were back here too. I'm going to go to bed in a minute, I will leave the door unlocked for you.

I place my phone down and start scrolling through the list of names and dates. My phone pings again.

No you fuckin' won't. I will sleep at my place tonight. Lock the fuck up!

I laugh whilst reading his message. I smile. Biting my lip I type my reply.

What if I don't do as I'm told? Will you punish me?

Less than thirty seconds later my phone alerts me to his reply.

I'm now sitting in a hospital waiting room with my fuckin' family and I'm getting hard thinking of all the ways I can punish your beautiful body.

I laugh to myself. Switching off my laptop I lock up and head up to bed. Once I've washed my face and brushed my teeth I send him a text goodnight.

I've been good this time. I've locked up. I'm in bed but it feels empty and weird without you. I love you. Bring me breakfast in the morning? Xx

I put my phone on the nightstand and close my eyes and fall asleep.

I don't get a reply from Wes and he doesn't arrive the next morning with breakfast. I have a bad feeling in the pit of my stomach. What if something has happened to him? I hope his sister in law is okay. All of these awful thoughts run through my head. I've never wished for my phone to ring or notify me more. I contemplate ringing the hospital but I know they won't tell me anything. It would be a little creepy if Wes' new girlfriend was trying to track him down.

CHAPTER ELEVEN

Wes

I ride and ride until I get to Lake's Ridge. I swear I nearly lost my shit in the hospital waiting room. Khan referring to Serena as a bitch, fuck! I could have killed the mother fucker. I've never felt that much anger at someone before. He meant no harm by it, I know it's a biker term, but fuck! I didn't like it.

I needed to get out of there. Keeping up the lies is becoming suffocating. I hate lying to my family, to the club, to Serena.

I stare into the dark night sky, there's nothing but the sound of crickets. I know I have to tell her. I know I have to come clean to Serena, but I can't let the club know yet. If they find out who she is they will use her to get to Jesús. They will use her as a way in. They'll put her life in danger and I will not have that. Over my dead body will I ever let anything happen to her. Now that I've found her I don't plan on ever letting her go.

I read her text over and over again; those three words I never thought I would hear. I LOVE YOU. Three words I never expected or thought I would feel.

In less than twenty-one days I have fallen so deeply in love with a woman I didn't even know existed before. She is the only thing I breathe, want, and live for. I don't need anything else in my world, only her. It will only ever be her.

I sit for I don't know how long, completely alone with my thoughts, thinking of ways that I can break the news to Serena. I hope I can do it in a way that means she doesn't hate me forever for it.

I hear the sound of a bike approaching and sigh.

"Fuck." I mutter. I turn around to see which brother has found me.

Rubble.

He pulls up beside me and gets off of his bike, lighting a cigarette.

"So you finished throwing your little temper tantrum?" He teases.

"Fuck off man. You have no idea what the fuck is going on." I bite back.

He snorts. "Yeah and whose fuckin' fault is

that? I know you didn't want to be an official club member, a brother, but you are. Just because you don't wear the kutte. Rip treats you like one. We all treat you like a brother and you act like a fuckin' brother. So why don't you share with all of us what the fuck has got you so bent out of shape?"

I stand toe to toe with Rubble.

"Just fuck off okay. Go back to Rip and be a good little bitch and follow your orders. Just leave me the fuck out of it." I growl in his face.

He laughs.

"You really are pussy whipped. Man I bet she has some sweet pussy! Maybe when you're done with her I can have a go. I love nothing more than sinking my dick into some slut's cunt." He sneers.

I rear my fist back and hit him hard. His head whips to the side.

"Don't you ever fuckin' touch her or I will fuckin gut you!" I snap.

Rubble smiles and wipes the blood from his lip.

"Feel better for that do ya? Want another go? Come on man, I'm an open target!" Rubble smiles opening his arms out wide.

I turn to walk away.

"Yeah that's what I thought, you've gone

soft. Oh well, at least I'm hard. I bet I can make her scream my name." Rubble smirks.

I spin around and charge towards him. Before I can lay a hit Rubble hits me twice. He grabs me and throws me to the ground. I forget that the fucker has years of training under his belt.

"Fuck." I groan.

Rubble leans in.

"You have your back up yet you have people that will fight with you. We'll fuckin' fight for you too. Now you've got that out of your system, get the fuck up and face your problems head on. There ain't no problem that can't be solved by the Satan's Outlaws." He winks.

I get up and brush myself down. My lip is throbbing and I can already feel my eye beginning to swell.

"Thanks for this." I say, pointing to my eye.

Rubble shrugs as he lights another cigarette.

"That's what brothers are for. You needed the wake-up call."

I sigh and pinch the bridge of my nose.

"If I offload what's really going on it will cause more problems, more issues. I know someone will get hurt because of it. I have this feeling, it's like there's a storm brewing and it won't pass. It will fuckin' strike and it's gonna take casualties with it." I admit.

"Storms always pass, whatever shit they cause. You will always have the club and your family to help clean up. Now as much as I'm loving this little heart to heart I actually came to find your ass to tell you that you're an uncle. You need to get your ass back to the hospital before Rip tears you apart." Rubble smirks and slaps my back.

"Christ, I'm an uncle." I mutter.

We ride to the hospital and the wind in my face stings like a motherfucker. Rubble is right, as much as I hate it. I can't keep all of this under wraps for much longer. Sooner or later I'm going to need to come clean and figure out a new plan.

I walk past the family, ignoring their frowns at my busted up face. I only stop to ask them for the room number.

I find the room and knock on the door.

Blake swings the door open and frowns at my face.

"Don't ask. I deserved it." I mutter, pushing past him.

Lily smiles and then her face falls when she sees my face.

"Oh for God's sake. What happened? Can I not even have a baby without any drama? Jesus Wes, what have you got yourself involved with?"

She snaps whilst breast feeding.

"Err Lily, you want to cover yourself up a bit before yelling at me? All I could focus on then was your tit." I shrug.

She grabs a blanket, covers herself and the baby, and rolls her eyes. Blake slaps me around the back of the head.

"Fuck! I'm injured enough bro, I don't need anymore." I complain.

"Oh shut up. You asked for that." Lily states.

"Fair point." I shrug.

"So come on, what have you got yourself involved with? Why have you been so absent? I was close to putting your goddamn picture on a milk carton." Blake asks.

I look at him and Lily; they're both waiting for my answer. I do want to tell them but now isn't the time. I'm not about to shit all over their happiness.

"It doesn't matter. It's nothing I can't handle. So you gonna introduce me to my niece or what?" I ask, hoping it's enough of a distraction for them to drop it.

Lily smiles. She covers herself and holds out my niece.

"Wes, meet Ivy." Lily beams.

I carefully take her in my arms. She's so tiny and delicate. I've never held a baby this small before and I'm worried I'll hurt her. She flutters her eyes open and looks at me.

"Shit, Blake we're gonna end up in jail for this little lady." I smile.

"Ain't that the truth." Blake laughs.

I stroke my finger over her tiny hand and she grabs it and holds it tight. Warmth spreads through my chest. I look at Blake. He smiles and nods, knowing exactly what I'm feeling. Having grown up without parents, holding little Ivy in my arms gives me an overwhelming feeling of love and protectiveness. I know that Blake and I will never let anything happen to her. We will always protect her.

I catch Lily taking a picture on her phone. I raise my eyebrow in question.

"You look adorable holding her. You can see the love in your face. I know she is going to be so well loved and protected. Poor girl is never going to get a date." Lily giggles.

"She can date when she's thirty, ain't no little shit going near her until then." Blake states.

I nod in agreement.

"Damn straight. They will have to go through us first. Plus I think the whole Satan's Outlaw biker family will scare off any potential assholes." I laugh.

Lily groans and shakes her head but I catch the small smile playing on her lips.

I hand her back to Blake.

"I have to get going. I will come by and see you soon, I promise." I lean over and kiss Lily on the head.

"You better. Don't make me hunt you down." She winks.

Blake follows me out. "You sure you're good?" He asks.

I try to easy his worries.

"Yeah I'm good. Everything is good." I smile.

His eyes search my face, he's not convinced. I sigh.

"I promise I'm fine, better than fine. I just have some things that I need to figure out, that's all. Stop worrying about me and focus on your new family, they need you more than me." I state before turning and leaving.

I go back to my place. Rubble is still staying in that rented house and keeping watch over the Cartel's house. As I lay in my bed my mind fills with thoughts of Serena, I wouldn't expect anything less, the woman owns me. Drained from the day I soon fall asleep.

****

The next morning I wake up late. My phone is dead, no power to ring Serena and I left my power cable at her house. I lay for a moment, trying to think of how to tell her. There's no other way around it. If I am going to tell her then it has to be now. I've already kept it hidden from her for too long, at least if she knows everything she can stay away from him. I can keep her safe and hidden from the Cartel.

I shower and get changed, deciding to grab some flowers on the way. What is it that they always say? You know when a guy has done wrong because he buys flowers. I've become a fuckin' cliché.

By the time I ride over it's the afternoon. I pull up and notice her car is gone. I walk up to the front door and try to open it: locked.

"Fuck." I grit.

I have no way of knowing where she is because my phone is dead. There is only one thing for it. I will have to sit on her step and wait. She has no family to go to so I have to hope she won't be long.

She is already pissed at me. This is not the best situation to be in right before you tell the woman you love that you've been lying to her since you met her.

CHAPTER TWELVE

Serena

I have to get out of the house; I can't carry on sitting around waiting for him to come back or for him to text or call. I'm angry, upset, and worried. This situation has only highlighted how little I know about him.

Maybe this was only meant to be a whirlwind romance. Maybe me falling head over heels for him so soon has scared him off. These questions just keep swirling around my head. This whole relationship thing is new to me and I have no idea what I'm supposed to do in situations like this.

I visit the retirement home to give them some more fresh flowers. I'll try anything to keep myself busy and keep my mind off of Wes.

I buy myself some dinner and don't arrive home until dusk. I pull up on the driveway and see Wes' bike. I look up and see Wes sitting on my front step with flowers in his hand, leant against the door and fast asleep. I smile to myself; it appears he's been waiting a while for me. Now he has had a taste of his own medicine.

I purposely slam the car door which makes him jump awake. He rubs his face. When I reach him I look at him and cross my arms over my chest.

He reaches out and tucks a strand of hair behind my ear.

"I'm so sorry I didn't call." He apologises.

I brush his hand away and move past him, not saying anything. I unlock the door and walk inside. I leave the door open for him to follow.

"Angel, please hear me out. I need you to know that I wanted to text or call you but I couldn't. My phone was dead and I left my power cable here. See?" He states, pointing to the socket in the living room. Sure enough, there is his power cable.

"Fine, apology accepted. You could have came over sooner rather than leaving me questioning everything and worrying all day that you were lying dead in a ditch somewhere." I point out.

"You're right, I'm sorry. I slept in late and by the time I got over here you were gone. Here, I got these for you." He hands me a bunch of flowers.

I give him a small smile and sigh.

"Look Wes, I'm new to this whole relationship thing. I know that things are moving quickly for us and things are intense. I would understand if you wanted to slow it down maybe take some time apart? I'd get it." I say, acting as though that I would be okay with that when in reality each word makes me feel like my heart is being squeezed.

Wes takes the flowers from my hand and chucks them onto the counter. He moves close to me until his body is pressed up against mine. I grip the counter to steady myself.

"You want me to leave? You want us to take a break and slow things down?" He asks softly.

I look down to the ground. He takes my chin and makes me look into his eyes.

"Angel, the truth?" He demands.

I bite my lip and shake my head. He runs his thumb across my lips.

"Kiss me." He whispers across my mouth.

I lean up and kiss him. Wes moans. His hands grab the back of my head as his tongue strokes against mine.

He slow the kiss and leans his head against mine, closing his eyes and cupping my face.

"We need to talk, there's something you

need to know." He admits. He opens his eyes and he looks almost scared.

"What is it Wes?" I ask, my voice wavering with nerves. Never in the history of someone saying 'we need to talk' has it ever been a good thing.

He steps back and takes my hand, leading me to the dining table. We sit and Wes doesn't let go of my hand. He continuously strokes his thumb across the back of my hand.

"Wes." I prompt.

"Okay, fuck. I hope you don't hate me after this." He sighs. "I know who your real father is, or rather, was. I've known this whole time. I also know that you have a brother." He admits.

I suck in a sharp breath and yank my hand from his.

"You've known the entire time we've been together and you never said anything to me! Why would you lie to me?" I ask, feeling my anger rise.

"You need to listen to me. You need to understand why I kept it from you. I had good reasons." He pleads.

"Then please enlighten me!" I snap.

"Okay. Your dad is a man called Luis, he was the head of the Mexican Cartel. He trafficked women and drugs and he murdered people. I'm sorry angel, he was not a nice man." He informs me.

I shake my head.

"No, you're wrong. There is no way my mama would be with a man like that, no way. She was an honest God loving Catholic. She always warned me about staying away from boys who weren't Italian and I can see why! You are full of lies!" I spit angrily. I walk to the fridge, grab a bottle of wine, and pour myself a glass. I take a long glug.

"Think about it Serena. Think about the letters, the whole 'my world' comments in it, the fact that your mom wouldn't let you near anyone who wasn't Italian. Don't you think that maybe she was worried you'd fall for someone like she did, someone that was wrong for her in every way." Wes points out.

"And yet her warnings were useless; I still fell for someone who is wrong for me in every way." I snap.

Wes smirks and shakes his head.

"You can say that all you want but I'm damn perfect for you and you know it. I met your fuckin' father. I met him because he kidnapped Rip's wife. I met him because we rescued lots of women and a child from his hideout. You can deny it all you want, but it's true." Wes yells.

I jolt.

"He kidnapped Rip's wife?" I whisper.

"Yeah he did." Wes answers.

"Did, um, did Rip kill him?" I ask.

Wes doesn't say anything so I take that as a yes.

"And my brother?" I ask.

Wes grits his jaw.

"Jesús…well…he's now the head of the cartel. He killed a prospect at the club too, he was just a kid. He wants war with the Satan's Outlaws. He's tried shooting at us, kidnap, double crossing us. He's hiding out right now and regrouping, planning. I still don't even know what he's got fuckin' planned. I've been following and watching the Cartel for a long time now. Please listen to me when I say do not go and see him. I've heard things and witnessed things he's done. He makes your father look like fuckin' Santa. Jesús isn't right in the head. He doesn't give a single shit about anyone. Didn't even care about his own mother. He's a cold hearted insane killer and he's someone you should never underestimate."

I sit back down. I put my head in my hands, feeling a headache coming on. My father was a criminal boss and now I found out my brother is the same but also insane. Then it occurs to me.

"You were following them to my store

weren't you?" I ask.

He sighs and nods.

"I watched them go to your store every week and buy flowers and throw them in the trash on their way out. I had no idea why they kept doing it. Then I saw you and you completely captivated me. I swear I felt my whole world change the moment I saw you. I had to meet you. At first I just assumed that maybe they liked you. You are a stunning woman after all. Then I saw the photo and you told me what you found out. That's when I knew why they were sniffing around. I don't think they know who you are yet but they definitely suspect something."

I down my glass and stand walking towards the sink.

"Mi hai mentito mamma! La mia vita è stata una bugia! (*You lied to me Mom! My life has been a lie.*)" I yell and throw my glass into the sink, smashing it.

Wes comes up behind me and pulls me into his arms. I sob.

"It's okay, I've got you." He soothes.

I lean back and wipe my eyes.

"Everyone I've ever loved has lied to me." I whisper.

Wes shakes his head.

"No. Your brother never did. I'm sorry I lied to you angel, I really am, but I didn't know how else to protect you. I didn't want to cause this." He says as he wipes my tears. "I didn't want to cause you any pain. I love you and I hate that I'm the one who has hurt you."

I give him a small smile and sigh.

"I'm going to run myself a bath. I need to be alone for a bit." I state as I move around him and head upstairs.

I lay in the bath, a million thoughts going through my head. My entire life has been based on a lie. Even after my mother died that lie continued. As much as I want to be angry at Wes, I can understand why he hid it from me. I just wish that he could've told me sooner.

His family are going to hate me, I'm related to the enemy, to the one who kidnapped the president of the Satan's Outlaws' wife! Fuck! No wonder Wes tried to keep his family under wraps.

Getting out of the bath I dry myself off. I'm so thankful that I have a beautiful bathtub to help soak the stress away. I put on my robe and open the bathroom door. I look around my bathroom and then it occurs to me.

Mamma told us our father had disappeared, that he had left me this house. Is this house Luis'? Is my house owned by the Cartel?

I walk downstairs. Opening the cupboard under the stairs and pull out my box of paperwork. I go through it, looking for the deeds to the house.

"What is it?" Wes asks, frowning.

"My father left me this house. My Mamma said it was a gift from my father." I state, still desperately trying to find the deeds.

"Shit." Wes sighs.

Finally I find the paperwork and read through it. I breathe happy, that Luis isn't on there.

Wes sits beside and takes the paper and reads it.

"So you own this house, you don't rent it?" He asks.

"Yeah, well, kind of. Its all a bit confusing." I state.

"Tell me everything." Wes demands.

"Okay. My mamma said that this house was left for me by my father but I have to pay rent to live here to prove that I am responsible enough to take care of my own home or something like that. There's a direct payment every month from my bank account. I'm not even sure where it goes. I assumed it went to the mortgage company or the bank or something?" I shrug.

Wes doesn't say anything, he just pulls his phone out and takes a photograph of the name on the papers.

"Show me the details on your account." He orders. I grab my phone and scroll through my transactions until I find it. He takes a photo of it and then hands me my phone back.

Wes takes me by surprise and pulls me into his arms.

"I promise I will get to the bottom of this." He says and kisses my head.

I sigh and lay my head on his chest. I hope he's right because the last thing I want is the Cartel knocking at my door.

"I knew my father wasn't a great man, that's why my mamma kept us away from him. I just had no idea how bad or that she loved him like that. I mean, do you think she knew about all of the bad things he did? All the things he has done?" I ask.

Wes strokes my hair and kisses the top of my head.

"Honestly, I don't know. The way you speak about your mom, I don't think she would even let herself near someone like that. But then love is the biggest emotion of them all. You don't own it or control it, love owns and controls you."

I look up at him as he cups my face.

"Would you not say that hate is the most powerful emotion?"

He smiles and shakes his head.

"Everything comes back down to love. Why do people seek vengeance? Well, it usually involved a loved one. Most crimes are crimes of passion. You ask any parent and they'll tell you they would kill for their children. I'd kill for you. I would lay my life down for you. I know that Blake and Rip, all of them, would do the same. Hate might boil and fester but you can guarantee that the hate was caused by love. Love can cause wars but it can also end them."

I lean into his hand and close my eyes.

"You keep saying that it's me who's going to kill you, but you are going to kill me. I love you so much it hurts. You're killing me with your words." I say, opening my eyes.

We stare at each other silently for a moment.

"Say something." I whisper.

"I'm taking you upstairs and fucking you right now." Wes declares and takes my hand, leading me upstairs.

CHAPTER THIRTEEN

Wes

It's a week later and I'm still no closer to finding out who is on her house documents. I lay awake. Serena is sprawled across me with her arms and legs wrapped around me like a spider monkey. I smile and stroke her hair. She moans and lifts her head off of my chest. She smiles, she's all cute and sleepy.

"Morning." She yawns, stretching and making the cover slip down, exposing her naked body.

I move quickly which makes her scream and laugh. I roll her onto her back.

"Hhmm, you're very eager this morning." She smiles.

"I've told you I can't control myself when I'm around you. Feel what you do to me." I rasp as I grab her hand and wrap it around my hard cock.

She smiles and bites her bottom lip.

"Well I suppose it's only fair you feel what you do to me." She whispers, placing my cock at her wet and waiting entrance.

"Fuck." I groan as I slide into her. I watch as her lips part. Her eyes become hooded as I enter her.

"Stunning." I rasp.

I lean down and take her mouth as I slowly glide in and out of her. Her nails scrape down my back. Suddenly there's a loud knocking at the front door. We pause.

"It's probably just a sales person. Ignore it. I need you to ignore it." Serena moans, lifts her hips, and clenches her walls around me.

I groan and turn my attention back to her. I start moving just as they knock again, this time louder and harder.

"Angel, that ain't no sales call. Stay here." I order.

"Well whoever it is, they better have a decent reason for disturbing us!" She fumes.

Smirking I lean over and kiss her.

"We can make up for it later." I whisper across her lips.

There's more banging.

"Stay the fuck here." I warn. She nods, looking concerned at my warning.

I pull on my jeans and t-shirt and grab my gun from my bag. I walk down to the front door and look through the peephole. It's Blake.

I sigh and open the door.

"What the fuck are you guys doing here?" I ask.

It's not just Blake, Lily is here too with their baby daughter Ivy.

"Don't you start with me Wesley Stone!" Lily fumes and storms past me.

I look to Blake who smirks. That fucker is happy to see me get my balls chewed out by his woman.

"You had this coming brother. She's not happy with you and, well, I'm not about to stop her. She isn't the only one that's pissed at you. You better listen to what she has to say." Blake warns. He pats my chest as he walks in carrying the baby in a car seat and a bag that looks like it has enough crap in for them to elope to another country.

I stand and take what she has to say. I have a shit load of respect for Lily; she's been through hell and back and still come out a strong woman. Plus when she loses her shit it's entertaining as fuck.

It goes on for a while and I barely say a word. Then the rest of the family turn up, which

I should have predicted would happen. Wherever there's one Rocke sister, there's another.

I explain to them what has been happening, what is going down. Serena is too nervous to come down which I don't blame her for. They are a rowdy bunch. They're loving and loyal but damn they're loud.

I should have known it would only be a matter of time before they found me. Rip has contacts who can find this shit out. I just hope the Cartel don't have people that could find this place.

I say goodbye to them and the last to leave is Daisy. She turns to me at the doorstep and smiles brightly.

"I'm so happy to see that you're happy Wes. Come and see us soon, okay? Oh and I almost forgot. Here." She says, handing me an envelope. It's an invitation to a party.

"What's this?" I ask.

"It's a celebration of our marriage." She whispers.

I stare stunned.

"Fuck! You know your sisters are going to kill you right?" I point out. "I can't believe you guys got married in secret. You're very brave little wallflower." I smirk.

Daisy smiles and places her finger to her

lips. "Shhhh! No one knows and we aren't announcing anything until the party. With everything that's gone on we just waited and waited. I didn't want a big fancy wedding, I wanted something that was personal and relaxed and felt like…" She pause and sighs. "Like I don't know… just us, just me and him and no crazy stuff. It was perfect. We can have this celebration with everyone we love now that things have calmed down a little. They will get over it. Plus I'm a tough cookie, didn't you know that?" Daisy laughs.

I laugh. She jokes about it but she really is. She is unbelievable.

"Well you have over a month yet and you got the first invite. So just make sure you and your lady are there. Maybe we will get to find out her name and see her face before then?" Daisy asks, her eyebrow raised.

I smile and pull her into my arms and kiss the top of her head.

"You can let go of my woman now." Carter yells from the end of the drive.

I smile and flip him off. Daisy laughs.

"I will be there, I promise." I whisper in her ear.

She smiles and squeeze me in a tight hug before running to Carter. He waves over his shoulder as he wraps his arm around her.

I shake my head and close the front door. I turn to walk upstairs and see Serena in her dressing gown.

"That was your family?" She asks.

I nod and smile. I walk to her and pull her into my arms.

"Yeah, that's them. They hunted and tracked me down." I smirk.

"I should have came down and introduced myself. They probably think I'm taking you away from them and that's not to mention all of the Cartel stuff." She shrugs.

"No way was that a good time to come and meet the family. They, um, well they had a few things to get off of their chests. I needed to have that shit thrown at me. If you were down here too you would've caught some of that shit and none of this is your fault. It's all on me and the way I've dealt with the situation."

Serena gives me a small smile and nods.

"Plus, they still don't know your name. I would prefer to keep it that way just a little longer. There is no telling what the Rocke women will do to you when they get their hands on you. They'll have you doing tequila shots within minutes." I laugh.

"Well didn't you hear? I'm half Mexican, so I can handle my tequila." Serena states wiggling her eyebrows.

I throw my head back and laugh. My laughter dies when she unties her robe and lets it fall to the floor. She takes my hand in hers and leads me back upstairs.

"Now Mr Stone, there's something you started earlier that you really need to finish." She purrs.

"Well I am a man of my word. I never leave a job unfinished." I wink, making her laugh.

CHAPTER FOURTEEN

Serena

I'm pottering in my garden watering my flowers and plants. I've had the most incredible month with Wes; we've basically not left the house. We probably spent eighty percent of the month in bed. I've loved every moment but now I need to go back to my shop. I need to get my business going again. If I don't I could lose it all and I've worked too hard for that to happen.

"Wes." I call as I carry on watering my flowers.

"What is it angel?" He answers from the sun lounger.

"Um, I need to go back to the shop. I need to reopen. I've already lost a huge amount of money having this past month off. If I lose any more my savings will disappear completely." I say while keeping my back to him and watering my flowers.

He makes me jump by coming to stand behind me. He wraps his arms around my waist and rests his chin on my shoulder.

"I knew we couldn't do this forever. Of course you can open the store, but only with some conditions." He states.

"Oh well thank you sir. Thank you for allowing me to open my own store. Tu dittatore!" I say sarcastically.

Wes growls and spins me in his arms, making me drop the watering can.

"One, I'm not a dictator. I need you to follow some rules to keep you safe. Two, I fuckin' love it when you talk Italian to me, even when you are throwing insults." Wes smiles.

I sigh and roll my eyes.

"Fine. Tell me which safety guidelines I have to follow."

"Fuck me, you're gonna be a pain in my ass." Wes states. I smile and shrug.

"Just hear me out. I will be at the shop with you for most of the day. When I am not with you I will be looking into the Cartel, aka your brother. You will not be alone for more than an hour. If for some reason I run over I will send Rubble to come and sit with you in the shop." He orders.

"I really don't think any trouble is going to

come of this. I think maybe the guys that visited me just wanted to make sure I knew nothing about my father and brother, which I didn't at the time." I point out.

"Just for my peace of mind, please just put up with it. I've seen shit happen and I'm not risking anything happening to you. The Satan's Outlaws, my family, will all know who you are soon and when that happens the Cartel will associate you with us. Please, I'm just trying to keep you safe." He says sincerely. He cups my face.

"Okay. I promise I do follow everything you say. Thank you. Now I'm going to cook our dinner. We should get an early night since my alarm will wake us up at 4am." I say as I place a quick kiss on his mouth and walk into the house.

"4am?!" Wes bellows after me.

I laugh.

"Yep. The market opens at 5am and I need to restock most of my store."

"Fuck." He groans.

****

The next morning Wes drives us to the market. The whole way there he groans about how it isn't natural to be up this early.

The flower market is alive with people shouting and walking around with their boxes filled with all of the different flowers and plants.

"Morning my gorgeous girl. I'm glad to see you back." Fred greets. He's the guy that I buy the majority of my stock from.

His eyes flicker to Wes and he smiles.

"Ah, I can see why you've been away." He winks.

"Fred, this is Wes. Wes, this is Fred, my main supplier for the shop. He gives me the best deals." I wink.

"Good to meet you." Wes greets, shaking his hand.

Fred nods.

"Likewise." He returns. He looks to me.

"You get those prices because you brighten up my day with your beautiful smile." Fred teases, holding his hands over his heart.

I laugh and shake my head.

"You're too kind Fred. Now, what have you got for me today?" I ask, rubbing my hands together.

Fred walks me though his stock and I pretty much take the load from him. Wes carries the bulk of it back to my car. The smell in the car ride over to the shop is amazing.

"Jesus I'm gonna smell like an old lady by the time I get out of this car." Wes grumbles.

"I'd still do ya." I tease.

"Of course you would! I'm a fuckin' catch." Wes quips back.

I laugh and shake my head.

We offload the flowers inside and I make quick work arranging them in the various stands. It's not as full as I would normally have it but it will do for now.

Wes' phone rings and whatever is said on the phone has him tensing.

"Fine. You have one hour of my time, that's it." He states before disconnecting.

"What's that all about?" I ask, leaning over and arranging the roses.

He sighs.

"I have to go for a meeting with Rip. Apparently there is something that needs to be discussed. I promise I won't be long. I will be back in no time. If you see those guys from the Cartel you call me straight away. I mean it. Don't even hesitate for a fuckin' second." He leans in and kisses me, pausing for confirmation.

"I promise."

He sighs before kissing me once again and leaving.

I have a ball of nerves swirling around my stomach when I unlock the door and switch the sign to open. I pray that they don't come in because I'm not sure I would be able to keep my cool until Wes arrived; I don't have a very good poker face. They would see right through me and know something is up.

I pop out back to make a coffee and hear the bell above the door chime as customers enter.

Carrying my coffee I see four women come in, one with a baby strapped to her front. They are all whispering and looking at me, not the flowers.

"Hi, can I help you with something?" I ask smiling.

"Well shit! Would you look at those lips?! Jesus, I bet you suck like a vacuum." One of the women states.

"Excuse me?!" I ask, affronted.

"Rose for God's sake! Keep your thoughts to yourself. You don't have to voice everything." One of the other women chastises.

She walks towards me and holds out her hand. "Hi, I'm Daisy. It's a pleasure to meet you." She smiles.

I shake her hand.

"Hi?"

"Good to know he hasn't talked too much about us." The one with the baby adds.

"I mean we are all very dysfunctional.

Wouldn't you keep quiet if we were your family?!" The one that looks like a biker laughs.

"Holy shit, you're them?! Err...I mean... Lily?" I say, pointing to the one with the baby.

She smiles and waves.

"Um, Rose?" I ask, pointing to the pretty one with no filter.

"I'm sorry, he didn't mention your name." I apologise to the biker.

"It's Patty, don't worry yourself about it." She smiles.

"And yes, of course! Daisy!" I smile at the sweet one in front of me.

"Of course she heard about Daisy. She's the special one." Rose states and rolls her eyes.

"Hey, he mentioned me too so that makes me special." Lily adds.

"You're married to his brother, it would be weird if he didn't mention you." Patty points out.

"Um, do you guys want a coffee or are you here to buy flowers?" I ask.

"Oh, well, we actually aren't supposed to be here. See Rose is married to Rip, the president of the Satan's Outlaws. She may have given him a little something something to get your name out of him. When Rose told Daisy that your name is Serena she knew immediately that this is where you work." Lily informs me.

"I know how to make my man crack, sometimes all you have to do is this thing with your tongue and…"

"Enough! I don't need those visuals this early in the day." Patty moans, interrupting Rose.

"I'm not sure if you remember me? I came here once before with Carter." Daisy adds.

I look at her and my memory hits me.

"Of course! You were looking for someone, right?" I ask.

Daisy responds, giving me a tight nod.

"So here is the thing: we know Luis was your daddy." Rose states.

I feel my cheeks heat with embarrassment and brace for confrontation.

"He was a dick of massive proportions, but you're not your father. We are having a cookout tomorrow night and we would like you to be there. It's a family one so no freaky shit will be going down. Wes will definitely say no and want to protect you from us. Fuck knows why because we're a delight!" Rose rants on.

"But you seem cool. I can't see you trafficking women and children, far too nice and pretty for that shit. Plus if Wes says you're good, you're good. He's a good guy and we love and trust what he has to say." Rose shrugs.

"He's the best." I sigh.

"Oh yeah, she is totally gone." Lily notes.

"So tomorrow night at 7pm, at the club. Tell Wes how much you want to come and he will have to bring you." Daisy adds smiling.

"We have to go before the prospect finds us and grasses us in. We gave him the slip a minute ago." Rose adds.

"Okay well thanks for the invite. Nice meeting y'all." I say, holding back my laughter as they all creep out of my shop, being careful not to be caught by whatever a prospect is.

So tomorrow I get to meet the family! I wonder how Wes will take that news. I feel better having met some of them but I can't deny that I'm still a little scared to meet the rest of them. I mean there's his aunt and uncle who are like parents to him and then there are Rip and the rest of the club members. Surely not all of them are going to welcome me with open arms?

CHAPTER FIFTEEN

Wes

I feel agitated and pissed off and I just want to get back to Serena. I didn't want to leave her in the first place, especially on her first day back at the shop.

I pull up at the club and head straight to church for the meeting.

When I open the door I find all of the Satan's Outlaws sitting around the table waiting for me.

"What the fuck is going on?" I ask

"I've filled in the brothers, they know what you and Rubble have been doing. Rubble came back with some intel last night and, well, it's too important to keep quiet any longer. This shit is getting real and war is close." Rip states whilst lighting his cigarette.

"Fuck." I sigh.

"Fuck is right. The DEA are watching them.

They're taking out the smaller players in Mexico. Soon they'll be after the bigger players and I do not need them sniffing around here. Oh and that's not all. They've had shipments delivered, weapons and men." Rip grits.

"What? They using minors to come and fight for them or what?" Mammoth asks.

Rips shakes his head.

"Not far off brother, eighteen year olds. From what we've heard, families in debt are forced to send their sons or brothers to fight for the Cartel. I'm not sure what numbers he has but I can guarantee it's more than what we have."

"So where the fuck does that leave us?" Khan grits angrily.

"It means I'm going back to Dreads for a meeting. I need to see if he wants to put his men on the line to fight Jesús." Rip rubs his jaw.

"He has helped us out in the past, why wouldn't he help us out now?" Rubble asks.

I nod in agreement. Dreads is a big player. He's a smart, cold, and calculated man. He knows that if the Cartel move in on this patch he loses out on customers and his reputation will be on the line.

"There is definitely enough to make him want to help us but it's still a big ask. He has the other option too, he could make a deal with the

Cartel." Rip states.

"What about asking the other chapters to come in and help out? We did it for the Louisiana chapter. Surely they can send a few of their guys down to us?" I point out.

"Yeah maybe. Their club is on the line at the moment. Their President is playing it risky and men are getting killed because of his bad decision making. I'd rather not have that shit added to our already sky high fuckin' problems." Rip sighs, taking a long pull on his cigarette.

"So what is the fuckin' plan Rip? Fuck! You're saying we're basically sitting fuckin' ducks! We just have to wait for the war to hit us and hope that Dreads helps us? We sound like whiney little bitches who can't handle our own shit. The Satan's Outlaws used to be feared and now we're fearing the goddamn Cartel! Why can't we take the war to them? Surprise the shit out of them?!" I fume.

Rip stands quickly. His ice cold glare is aimed at me and his jaw is tensed so hard it looks like it could snap.

"I'll remind you that you ain't even an official brother and sitting in on these meetings is a damn privilege! Call us whiney little bitches again and I will gut you. I don't give a shit that you're my cousin, I will not have my fuckin' club disrespected in that way." He growls.

I give him a tight nod and he sits back down.

"Now apart from most of the bullshit Wes has said, he isn't wrong. There is a chance that we will take the war to him, it's the only way we can outplay them. There is one more thing: not one member of the cartel can be alive after this. The only way to end this shit is to end them. If we don't get rid of them, they will just keep on coming for us. I'm still going to meet with Dreads though, he's an ally to us and I like to think he prefers us to the fuckin' Cartel." Rip states.

Rip's phone rings and he answers it.

"Yeah." He lets out a sigh and pinches the bridge of his nose. "Yeah. Fuck sake." He says as he disconnects.

"What?" I ask.

"Rose and the rest of them gave their prospect the slip and now he can't find them." He smirks, shaking his head.

"Why are you fucking laughing? Aren't you at least a bit worried that the Cartel have taken them?" I ask.

His gaze comes to me and he laughs and shakes his head.

"Think about it. What on earth would make them want to give the prospect the slip? Who are they dying to fuckin' meet?"

It hits me.

"Oh fuck, Serena." I mumble.

"Got it in one." Rip laughs.

"But how did you find out her name? How did they find out her name?" I ask.

"Come on, I ain't stupid. I've know for a while who she is. As for the women, well, Rose used her powers against me last night. I might try and keep more shit from her in the future just so she can do that to me again." Rip laughs.

The rest of the brothers laugh and I can't help but smirk.

"Fuck. I better call Serena and make sure they haven't ambushed her and scared the shit out of her." I mutter.

"Wes." Rip calls before I leave. I turn to face him. "We will make sure she is okay. You know that right? We know what's coming this time and we can prepare. I promise we won't let anything happen to her, to any of them. I'd lay down my own fuckin' life." He states vehemently.

"I know." I nod and leave, calling Serena on my way out.

"Hello?"

"Angel."

"Hey, is everything okay?" She asks.

"Yeah I'm just checking you're not running

and screaming from my crazy family." I smirk.

"No, they were lovely. Maybe only a little bit scary. They mentioned a cookout tomorrow night. They said that you have to take me." She states.

"Oh fuck, fine. I swear if any of the brothers even look at you I will not hold myself back."

"They said it was just a family one, nothing freaky." She laughs.

"Jesus! Okay but you stay by my side. I know what they will be like when they see you, when a woman doesn't wear a man's kutte at a cookout she is fair game. It happened with Lily and Rose. Always ends with fists flying." I admit.

"Oh. Okay, I promise not to leave your side."

"Good. I'm on my way to you now. See you in a bit."

"Okay. See you in a bit." She repeats back to me.

"Angel, say the words." I demand.

"I love you." She whispers.

"Fuck. I will never get tired of hearing those words leave that beautiful mouth of yours. Love you too." I reply before disconnecting.

"Glad you've found that, man."

I turn on my heel and see Mammoth with his arms crossed over his broad chest, watching me.

"Thanks." I reply.

"Don't let it go. Trust me man, I messed my one chance up. Regret is a powerful thing that will eat you up inside. I regret every damn day that I let her go." He states.

"I don't plan on it." I yell over my shoulder as I open the car door. I pause.

"Hey Mammoth." I yell.

He turns around to face me. "Never too late to right those wrongs. Never too late to get on your knees and beg for forgiveness. If she means that much to you, go for it." I don't wait to hear his response. He salutes me as I drive off.

****

"Just wear whatever makes you comfortable, it's just a cookout." I yell. I'm at the bottom of the stairs waiting for her.

"It's not just a cookout, it's a cookout with your family!" She yells back.

"Christ! Fine, but we have to get going." I yell back.

I would rather not go at all. I know I'm

going to have my ass chewed out by the brothers and the rest of the family.

Serena walks down the stairs in a long black maxi skirt with splits either side that stop mid-thigh, and a white loose fitting cropped t-shirt showing a snippet of her beautiful olive stomach. She also has on her silver bangles and necklaces.

"Fuck I'm in trouble." I mumble.

"Oh, now why would that be?" She says, fluttering her eyelashes, knowing full well why.

"Don't play me angel, you know what that will get you." I growl.

"Oh I know! The more I play the more fun my reward is." She winks, walking out of the door to the car, swaying her hips purposefully and smiling at me over her shoulder. I've said it before and I will say it again: that woman is going to kill me!

I park up at the clubhouse and open Serena's door for her. I hold her hand as we walk around to the cookout.

As we walk around the bend the guys all cheer and wolf whistle.

"Fuck off." I yell back. Serena hides her face in my chest, clearly embarrassed.

"Well, it's about time. Were you going to keep her hidden from us forever?" Aunt Trudy states, pulling Serena from my arms and into a hug.

"Welcome to the family my girl! Let's introduce you to everyone." She states as she pulls Serena away to meet everyone.

"Err, nice to meet you." Serena calls out. I smile and shake my head.

"Suck me sideways! She is one fuckin' hot bitch." Khan states, handing me a beer.

"You not learnt from the last time? Call her that again and I will hand you your ass." I threaten.

"My bad brother, old habits and all that. Seriously though I can see why you're so protective over her." Khan adds.

"You know the Rocke sisters want to take her out? I overheard Lily mention the word tequila. Just giving you a heads up." Blake states as he walks up to me.

I ignore him; I'm too busy watching as our aunt throws Serena in the deep end and introduces her to everyone.

"I see Ma stole her from you. That must be a new record! How long was she here? Like thirty seconds?" Rip jokes, walking up to us. "I also heard Rose arranging a girls night and Serena is the main focus, so prepare yourself for that." Rip warns.

I still don't respond. I'm far too captivated watching Serena laugh and smile. She hugs my uncle Max.

"Good to see your face Wes. You guys heard about this damn tequila night? Patience has told me they're arranging it for Saturday. You better prepare for the hangovers the next day." Axel states, having a pull of his beer.

"Daisy mentioned it too. Shit, it never ends well." Carter adds.

"I'm not having them go out to a bar at the moment, not with the way things are. They can do it here in the clubhouse. At least that way I can keep an eye on them and make sure they stay out of trouble." Rip states.

"They never stay out of trouble." I remind him, my eyes still firmly fixed on Serena.

"Man ain't that the truth. You can look away from her you know? She isn't about to disappear. She's safe here, you know that." Blake points out.

"Yeah and look what happened when you took your eyes of off Lily, Rose, even Patty. I don't plan on letting that happen." I state, facing them.

"Chill the fuck out man, she isn't made of damn china! Let her meet the family. She's safe, you're safe, it's all good." Carter points out.

I sigh, he's right, everyone here is family. This is not a normal cookout: the brothers are on their best behaviour and the kids are running around, it's all family.

"Man, I hate it when you fuckers are right." I laugh.

"Well then you must hate it a lot because I'm always fuckin' right." Blake smirks.

I chat to them for a while. It feels good having some normality with the dark cloud that is the Cartel hanging over my head. It's good to just forget for a while. I look for Serena and see her sitting with Lily, Rose, and Patty. She's laughing so hard that she's wiping the tears from her eyes. I look around and catch Rubble leaning against the wall, his eyes on Serena.

I walk to him.

"Don't fuckin' go there Brother." I warn.

His gaze flicks to mine.

"I would never fuckin' go there. Give me some credit. Can't help but admire her beauty, that's all." He states.

"Well just make sure that's all it fuckin' is." I bite back. I can see it in his eyes, he likes her. He likes what he sees. That doesn't settle too well for me.

"Oh my days Wes! Why on earth did you keep that girl hidden from us for all this time?!

She is such a beauty! Absolutely stunning. Isn't she Ben?" Penny, Lily's mother, says excitedly whilst pulling me in for a hug.

"Yeah, if I was twenty years younger." Ben, her husband, sighs.

Penny's head whips around.

"If you were twenty years younger you'd still be too bloody old for her. Don't behave like a dirty old pervert Ben! No one likes a pervert." She chastises.

I laugh as does Rubble. Ben looks to us and raises his eyebrow.

"So you can throw yourself at all of these guys, say how handsome they are and feel up their bloody biceps, but I can't comment on or appreciate a beautiful young woman?" he argues back.

"Good, now you get it." Penny states, patting his face and walking off.

"Bloody woman! She drives me up the wall. You know she's started taking a photography course? She wants all of you lot to take part in an erotic biker calendar for charity!" He exclaims.

"Fuck, that is not happening. I'm not flashing my junk for all to bloody see!" Rubble states, shaking his head.

"That's because you've got a small dick." Khan laughs, walking over to join us.

"Fuck off Khan, just because you flash your cock at any chance you get that doesn't mean we're all the same." Rip states.

We laugh.

"Hey, don't go hating on my magnificent cock. You shouldn't hide that kind of beauty. It deserves to be shared for all to enjoy!" Khan yells, thrusting his hips.

"What happens when you share your cock around too much Khan?! Huh? You get the mother fucking clap. For God's sake man, keep the bloody thing in your pants!" Rose yells.

Everyone bursts out laughing except for Khan who looks a little pissed off.

"You're a nurse! That shit is supposed to be confidential!" Khan yells back.

"Khan, she's the club nurse, it ain't no hospital or doctor's office. It's the old store-room. Jesus man, if you have the clap go to the actual hospital. Don't pull down your fuckin' trousers in front of my old lady." Rip points out.

Thankfully the rest of the cookout seems to go okay. Little Maddie and Caden run around like hellions while Miguel stays quiet, just watching them run, cuddled into Daisy.

I finally manage to steal Serena for a minute. I pull her around the corner and pin her up against a room and take her mouth.

"I needed your mouth, these lips. It's been too long, I've missed." I say between kisses.

"I haven't gone anywhere, I'm still here. We're at the same cookout." She sighs.

"Hhmm but I've had to share you. I don't like that. You're mine and I like to remind you of that." I say as I bite her neck.

She gasps.

"Always yours Wes. There will never be anyone else, just you."

I growl, feeling my dick harden and press painfully against the fly of my jeans. "Jesus, I want to fuck you right now."

"Later, not here. Oh and I'm going out with the girls tomorrow night. Can you handle a few hours without me?" She asks.

I cup her face and she smiles.

"Angel, it looks like I'm gonna have to. I will warn you though, you're in for a lot of tequila shots. Just don't get into trouble." I beg.

She frowns, confused.

"Why would I get into trouble?"

"Because those nights always attract trouble, believe me. There is always some kind of drama, even though you guys will be drinking here. Trust me, they always seem to end up in trouble." I laugh.

"Well now I'm nervous." She states and bites her bottom lip.

I lean in and kiss her.

"Don't be, you're in good hands, just brace for something. It could be anything! It could be exes, which you don't have, so that's good. It could be a guy coming onto you, then I'd have to kick his ass. Hell, at the end of it all, Daisy will give you a musical performance like no other." I laugh.

"A musical performance?" She asks curiously.

"Yeah. When Daisy gets shitfaced she sings everything and it's like a musical, like Disney on crack." I laugh.

"Wow. I guess I'm in for a fun night." She states. "The girls are coming around to mine to get ready at five. They said they will help me get my biker chic on. Whatever that means!" She shrugs.

"It means you're going to look all fuckin' hot in biker bitch clothes and I'm going to have to beat every fucker for eye fucking you. Yep, definitely going to be a night of drama. Hell." I sigh.

Serena laughs.

"Hey! There you two are. Get your asses round here!" Aunt Trudy yells.

I grab Serena's hand and lead her back to the chaos.

CHAPTER SIXTEEN

Serena

After the cookout last night I am both excited and nervous for what tonight will hold. I was so scared walking into the club to meet Wes' family and friends, worried they wouldn't like me, but they were so lovely and welcoming.

"What are you doing now?" Wes asks, walking into the kitchen while I'm quickly mopping the floor.

"Tidying up the house. The girls will be here in thirty minutes and I have to make sure the house is tidy before they arrive. I don't want them thinking I live in a shithole. I need to make a good impression. I'm new, they have to like me." I state, slightly out of breath from where I'm mopping so fast.

"Calm down. The house is immaculate and if there was an Olympic event for moping floors in record time I'm sure you'd fuckin' win. Just calm down. They will love you because I love you." Wes states and takes the mop from my hand before kissing me.

"Better?" He whispers across my lips.

"Hhmm hhmm." I hum in response.

Wes walks me back and lifts me onto the counter.

"Wes! What are you doing?" I gasp as his hands slide my skirt up to my hips and he moves my panties aside.

"We've got thirty minutes, that's more than enough time to make my angel feel better." He rasps as he slides himself inside me.

"Oh." I moan.

I place my hands on his shoulders and move my hips. He groans and I smile, looking up at him. I reach between us and start circling my clit. His eyes drop to my hand and he growls.

"I don't think so angel." He states, pulling out of me making me groan in disappointment. He pulls me down off of the counter and spins me around.

"Lean over the counter and spread those legs." He growls deep in his throat.

I do as he asks.

"Now, hands behind your back. I'm the one that will be giving you pleasure angel, it will be my cock, my hands, and my mouth. You only get to touch yourself when I say. Am I clear?" He whispers in my ear, his cock pressed teasingly at my entrance.

I nod.

"Answer me."

"Yes sir." I whisper.

"Good girl." He states as he slams into me hard, holding my wrists together at the small of my back. He pounds into me, his cock filling and stretching me. I feel my walls begin to tighten as my orgasm builds.

"Yes! Fuck. Wes!" I moan.

"You see how my cock fills you? Fuckin' perfect. It's fuckin' made for you." He groans.

He's relentless. He continues to slam himself inside me. My pleasure builds until I can't take it anymore.

"Oh God! Yes!" I cry out as my climax hits me. Wave after wave of pleasure takes over my body, making me shudder. My walls clamp around him, squeezing him, milking him.

"Fuck! You're so fuckin' tight. I can feel you milking my cock. I'm going to come in your tight pussy but not yet, I'm going to make you come again first." He grits through his teeth.

His hand connects with my behind, slapping it hard.

He reaches round and pinches my nipple, making me cry out. The pleasure shoots straight to between my legs.

"That's it angel, feel me, feel what I do to you." He pants.

His hand moves down my body and his fingers gently graze over my clit. I gasp and jolt at how sensitive it feels. He starts slamming inside of me again as his fingers circle my clit.

"Oh fuck Wes!" I cry as my legs start to shake.

"That's it, come for me. Scream my fucking name." He growls.

It hits me like a sudden bolt of lightning. My whole body tenses and it's almost too much. The pleasure is too much for my body to take.

"Wes! Fuck!" I scream.

"Fuck!" He growls, finding his own release.

Wes lets go of my wrists and rubs them gently. He pulls me up so I'm standing, still connected, still feeling wobbly. His hand wraps around my front while the other turns my face to his. He leans in, taking my mouth and kissing me softly.

"That was fuckin' incredible." He whispers.

"It really was. The only thing is, I'm not sure if I will be able to walk." I smile.

Wes smiles and kisses me again.

"I'm going to jump in the shower and get cleaned up." I state.

"Now I want to join you." He says, nipping my bottom lip.

"Well, you can't and the girls will be here soon. You need to let them in and start hosting for me." I state, pecking him on the lips before I walk upstairs.

"I can't believe you just walked away like that! You're really leaving me here in your kitchen with my cock out. Talk about use and fuckin' abuse. Geeze!" Wes teases.

I stop and lean over the banister.

"Oh yeah, I totally got mine." I yell, laughing as I continue walking up the stairs.

****

"Oh my fucking god you totally banged just before we came over didn't you?! I can smell the satisfaction of good sex a mile off." Rose accuses.

"Oh my god do I smell like sex?!" I ask, horrified. I try sniffing my clothes.

They all laugh.

"What?" I ask.

"Well now we know that you definitely did

have sex." Rose smirks.

"Oh my god you totally played me!" I laugh.

"Yeah and cheers to getting some dick in before the girls night!" Lily leans over and clinks our glasses.

"I always wondered if Wes was the dominant type and I guess this proves that he is." Rose states.

"How does sex before a girls night prove that Wes is the dominant type?" Daisy asks.

"Well he's marked his territory. He stated his claim and made his mark to all other men. It's animalistic, it's hot. It's almost like he is declaring to all of the other men not to go near you because you're his." Rose tells us before downing the last of her drink and then waving her empty glass in the air.

"Prospect, another round please!" She yells.

"Oh my god do I actually smell?!" I ask again, worried.

"No!" Daisy yells.

"Girl, you have an aura surrounding you. It's an 'I've just been thoroughly fucked by the man I love' type of aura." Rose smiles. I blush.

"If that's the case then you all have it too!" I point out. They each give each other side glances and laugh.

"Holy shit! Did we all get a pounding before we came out tonight?" Lily asks.

Each one of us nods.

"Holy crap! It's like a long distance orgy." Rose mumbles just as the young prospect brings us another tray of drinks.

I had to get Wes to explain all of the biker names and words. I was getting very confused at all of the different names for everyone.

"So come on then, spill. Is Wes all dominant and Mr Grey in the bedroom?" Patty asks.

I smile and bite my lip.

"A little, there's no whips or weird sex toys but he puts me in my place. He punishes me if I misbehave." I giggle.

"Holy shit! Tell us more." Patty says and they all lean forward. They're intrigued to hear about this side of Wes I guess.

"He spanks me if I misbehave, like leaving the door unlocked or, um, if I pleasure myself without his permission." I mutter, embarrassed.

"Well fuck me that's hot." Rose states.

"Who knew Wes would be like that in the bedroom!" Daisy shrugs.

Lily pours us all a shot of tequila and hands them out.

"To Serena and Wes and their kinky as fuck

sex life!" She yells, holding up her shot.

The girls all cheer and we down our shots. Feeling a little fuzzy in the head I stand to go to the bathroom and wobble a bit.

"Whoa easy!" Daisy yells, reaching for me.

"I'm good, I'm good. It's these ridiculously high heeled boots you put me in." I complain, looking down at the six inch spiked stiletto thigh high boots.

The girls arrived at mine with wine and a mini suitcase filled with clothes, shoes, and make up and got me all dressed up to go to the clubhouse.

They picked out a pair of skin-tight black acid wash jeans and a light almost dusky pink bodysuit. They paired them with these thigh high killer boots. I added my own jewellery and bangles and left my hair wavy.

I walk to the bathroom. I open the door to what I thought was the bathroom but it's a bedroom. I spy a door that looks like it leads to a personal bathroom. Desperate to relief myself I check behind me, quietly shut the door, and tiptoe into the bathroom.

After taking care of business I wash my hands and go to leave. I open the door and walk straight into a hard chest. I stumble backwards but strong hands reach out, grabbing me and pulling me flush to their body.

I look up and see Rubble. Embarrassment floods my cheeks, making them go bright red.

"Oh god! I'm sorry Rubble. I was desperate for the toilet and I got lost. I saw the bathroom and thought I could sneak in for a quick pee." I ramble out quickly.

I look down and realise my hands are splayed on his chest.

"Oops sorry." I say, removing my hands.

Rubble doesn't move or say anything, he just looks at me intently.

"Uh Rubble, you okay?" I ask.

He shakes his head and lets go. Moving to the side he holds his arm out for me to pass.

"Great, thanks. Um, sorry." I mumble as I scuttle past.

I return the table and the girls cheer, holding out another round of shots. Shit, this night is about to get messy!

"So, I said I may be a virgin but I'm an adult. I can make my own decisions. Just fuck me already!" I yell, waving my hands about and spilling drink everywhere.

"Men! They never listen, they're always wanting to protect us, thinking we are these delicate little flowers. Let me tell you, I could kill a man with my bare hands if I wanted to." Daisy giggles. "Ding dong the dick is dead!" She sings laughing.

The other exchange a look and I see Patty take her phone and send a text. She doesn't even seem to be that drunk.

"Hey how come, you aren't ine...inebr...inebriat...err...pissed." I slur.

"Because I'm a biker bitch. I was a biker brat born and raised and I can handle my alcohol pretty well." She smiles.

"So unfair!" Lily says, slumped in her chair throwing bits of napkin at a prospect who is holding a pint glass for her to try and get it into. It keeps hitting him on the head and every time it does, Lily just giggles.

"Jesus Christ, look at the state of them." We hear a deep voice say behind us.

We turn around and see Wes, Blake, Carter, Rip, and Axel watching us.

Lily is still too busy concentrating on getting a bit of napkin into a pint glass and hasn't even noticed them.

"Hi!" I smile and wave.

"Yes you mother fucking douche canoe! Get in there! Who's a legend? I'm a legend!" Lily yells, jumping up from her chair and dancing around. She goes up to the prospect and points in his face.

"Okay that's our cue to leave." Blake says, laughing.

He takes hold of Lily's hand and leads her out.

"Oh babe did you see my awesome trick shot?! Ooo wait, bye ladies!" She yells over her shoulder.

"Too-da-loo!" Daisy sings. "Until we meet again…" She starts singing.

"And we are done." Carter states, picking her up and carrying her out.

"Aww my knight in shining armour. Where have you been?!" She cries, hugging him.

"Well, I am off to get me some. Have a good night ladies." Patty says as she stands.

"La-la-la not listening. That's my brother. So disgusting." Rose complains with her hands over her ears.

"Sweetheart, get that fine ass over here and let's go." Rip orders.

"Don't tell me what to do. I will leave when I am ready to leave." Rose snaps while pouring another drink.

"Jesus Christ you're a pain in my ass." Rip mumbles.

"Oh well now I may stay for another drink

after this one, you know, if I'm so much of a pain in the ass to you." Rose says, flipping him off.

Rubble walks in just wearing a pair of jeans with no shirt.

"Hey, you guys want to keep it down? I'm trying to sleep." He complains.

"Sorry Rubble. Sorry for creeping in your room to pee." I yell.

"What?!" Wes yells and turns to face Rubble.

"I walked in and she had used my bathroom, that's all it was. Calm the fuck down man." Rubble brushes him off.

"Yeah, honestly I went to pee and then walked straight into him when I left. I nearly fell but Rubble is strong and moved super duper quick and grabbed hold of me tightly so I didn't fall." I say, blowing Rubble a kiss. I catch his lips twitching, fighting a smile.

Out of nowhere Wes' fist connects with Rubble's face and I watch as Rubble stumbles back, holding his nose. There is blood splattered across his face.

"Wes!" I yell.

"Stay the fuck out of it!" He yells back.

"Mother fucker what is your problem? You want me to kick your ass again because I will if I fucking have to." Rubble yells and spits blood on the floor.

"You know why I fuckin' hit you and you would have done the same if it was the other way around and you know it! She is mine so back the fuck off. Stop looking at her the way you do and don't fucking go near her!" Wes yells at Rubble.

Rubble's jaw tenses and his eyes flicker to mine before he turns and leaves to walk back to his room.

"Serena get your things, it's time to go." Wes says sharply.

"No." I answer back.

His gaze snaps to mine.

"Come on." He says softer.

"No, I'm staying with Rose and Rip. You can stay the hell away from me." I say, crossing my arms over my chest.

No way am I going anywhere near him tonight, hitting Rubble like that was out of order and he knows it. I'm not sure what Wes is getting at, Rubble has been nothing but polite and kind to me. He's never made a pass at me or said anything that would make anyone think that he liked me. Wes needs to know that I'm not some object he can own, I'm not going to be dictated to.

"Go brother. We will look after her tonight.

Go cool off." Rip says to Wes. I turn my back on Wes and pour another drink. He doesn't say anything else, he just leaves.

Rip and Rose show me to a room that apparently Wes uses sometimes if he stays at the clubhouse. I lay in the bed and close my eyes. I don't cry. I'm angry and disappointed at his behaviour. I'm tired and the alcohol soon helps me to drift off to sleep.

The next morning I stumble half asleep out of the room, the smell of breakfast cooking waking me up. I stand in the doorway and yawn and stretch.

"Uhh hum." A guy clears his throat.

I open my eyes, squinting as the headache from my hangover starts kicking in.

Rubble is standing there and his eyes aren't on my face. I look down and see I'm in my underwear.

"Shit!" I hiss, running back into the room and putting my clothes from last night back on.

I open the door and see Rubble with a smirk on his face, leaning against the wall.

"Why does it seem like every door I open you're on the other side?" I ask.

He shrugs. I go to walk past him but he grabs my hand, stopping me.

"Wes wasn't in the wrong for hitting me."

He states.

"What?" I ask on a whisper.

"He wasn't wrong, I was out of order even touching you. Fuck, I shouldn't even be looking at you like I do. He's right. I like you. You're unbelievably hot, probably one of the most beautiful women I've ever seen." He says, softly cupping my face.

I freeze, stunned, with a deer-caught-in-the-headlights expression on my face.

"I would never cross that line, Wes is a brother and you're his woman. That's all there is to it. I just thought you should know to go easy on Wes because I would have beat the shit out of him for doing exactly what I've done. He's a good guy, one of the best, so this is my fault." Rubble admits.

I go to say something but he continues.

"Maybe one taste of the forbidden fruit." He says softly as his thumb strokes my bottom lip. He leans down and kisses me quickly and softly. I don't kiss him back, I'm too stunned and taken aback by his admission.

"I will see you around." Rubble says quietly before turning and leaving.

"Err Rubble." I call after him.

He stops and turns.

"I appreciate you wanting to make things

right for me and Wes, but kiss me again and I will put your nuts in a vice. I'm with Wes and that's never going to change." I state before walking away to the kitchen.

I will never tell anyone about that encounter, I wouldn't drive that wedge between Wes and Rubble's friendship. What's done is done and we can all move on from it. My first mission now is to find that amazing smelling breakfast and some painkillers to kill this ridiculous headache.

CHAPTER SEVENTEEN

Wes

Spending the night without Serena by my side was hell but I get it. She was right, I did overreact, but she doesn't know Rubble. I have never seen him look at a woman like that before.

I head back to the club house deep in thought. I'm trying to figure out how I'm going to grovel and apologise my way out of this.

I notice a black SUV behind me and realise it has followed me all the way from Serena's place.

I pick up my cell and call Rip.

"She's fine." He answers.

"Good, but that's not why I'm calling. I've got a black SUV behind me that has been following me from Serena's place. I'm going to try and lose him but I may need some help giving him the slip if you and the guys can come out in your truck. I don't want to lead them to the clubhouse or they will know that Serena is involved with the club and that puts her even more in danger. We still don't know what he wants from her." I state.

"Leave it with me. Three of us have our trucks here. Where are you?" He asks.

"Bridge street." I answer.

Rip disconnects and I pull over. I park the car and pull on my cap. Keeping my head low I pretend to be fixing something in the engine. I notice the SUV pull up further down the road. They're watching me. I lean over the engine, hiding my phone out of sight, and text Rip to hurry the fuck up.

I hear the sound of engines approach and I look up to see three trucks coming down the road. It's the Satan's Outlaws with all of their licence plates removed so they can't be traced. I slam the hood shut and jump in, pulling out in front of the trucks. They cover me, hiding Serena's much smaller car. I check my rear view mirror and see the SUV trying to swerve around the trucks but the brothers are making it very difficult for them.

I turn left and then right and pull down a small side road between two houses and watch as the trucks and SUV pass by in my mirror. I reverse out and make my way to the club. That was close, too fuckin' close. They are practically hunting Serena now. I still don't understand why. From what I've heard Jesús isn't exactly the 'want your family close' type of guy. He celebrated when his father died by throwing a massive party with hookers and drugs.

We need to get to him before he gets to Serena. I park the car around the back of the club to make sure that if the Cartel drive by, they won't see her car. At the moment they don't know that she is connected to the Satan's Outlaws and I would like to keep it that way. It's safer for her and safer for the club.

I wait outside for the brothers to return. I'm too tense and uptight, I need to speak with them find out where if and where they lost them.

I don't have to wait long the trucks pull up, Rip, Mammoth and Khan jump out and walk straight towards the door.

"Church, now!" Rip yells as soon as we step inside.

We all walk in and wait. The brothers are exchanging looks and wondering what the fuck is going on. Rip is tense and pissed, everyone can feel it in the room. Rip lights a cigarette and chucks his blade on the table. It's covered in blood.

"Fuck." I snap.

"Fuck is right. They knew. They knew it was us. It was a fuckin' set up. They know everything Wes. They even know we've been watching them! How in the fuck do they know all of our fuckin' business?!" Rip roars angrily. He picks up his chair and throws it across the room. The brothers duck out of the way.

"Either the fuckers have been watching our every move or we have a mole. Now you know what we do to moles, I won't show any fuckin' mercy to anyone that betrays this club." Rip threatens, cracking his neck.

He's gone. His eyes are rabid. You can see he wants blood and so do I.

"He's been fucking Jesús sister, there's your fucking mole!" Fury yells and points to me.

I don't even think. I fly across the table and launch myself at him, hitting him over and over until the brothers pull me off of him.

"Enough! Fury stop being a fuckin' dick or I will beat you myself. Wes is the most loyal member we have. Serena has never met her father and she didn't even know about Jesús until Wes told her. Stop being a fuckin' moron." Rip sighs, pinching the bridge of his nose.

"They must have seen me with her." I state.

All eyes come to me.

"Think about it, it makes sense. They must have seen me with her and followed us here. A bit of research and they would've found out who

I was." I point out.

"Doesn't explain how they knew we were watching them. I didn't even tell half my men that. We have a different plan to make now, because they've just stepped up the game." Rip says whilst pouring himself a whiskey.

"Yeah. Now they're gonna figure out that three of their men are missing because of us." Khan smirks.

"What did you do with the bodies?" I ask.

"Set fire to their SUV." Mammoth crosses his arms over his chest.

"How long do you think we have until they retaliate?" Rubble asks.

Rip shrugs.

"I don't know? Fighting a war against Luis when he was in charge of the Cartel was easier because you could predict when he would act. Jesús is different, he doesn't follow rules. There is no honour with him, he is unpredictable. That's what makes him so fuckin' dangerous." Rip says and downs his whiskey.

"So now what? I ain't sitting here like a damn target." Max says.

"You know what it means. It means fucking lockdown. Get all of the family members in now. I am not risking anyone's life. I'm going to meet with Dreads within the hour. I will not lose any more fuckin' lives to the damn Cartel!" Rip slams down the gavel.

"I'm coming with you." I state.

"Fine but ring Blake. Get him, Lily, and Daisy in too. No matter how much they argue about it, they are coming in." Rip orders.

I nod and step outside to ring Blake.

"Hey what's up? Are you actually going to visit us?" Blake answers sarcastically.

"No man. Shit has just got real. Pack up your shit and head over to the club for lockdown. Ring Carter and get him and Daisy here too. No arguments." I state.

"Fuck. Okay, I'm on it. What about Penny and Ben?" He asks.

"Yeah everyone. Rip's close to losing his shit over it. I'm going with him to meet with Dreads. This is the war that's been coming for us." I state.

"Fuck, right. I will see you later." He says before disconnecting.

I walk in search of Serena. I need to see her to apologise and, most importantly, tell her what the fuck is going on.

I find her at the bar with Rose.

"Angel." I call.

She stops laughing and her eyes come to

mine. Slowly she walks to me, tucking her hair behind her ear and biting her lip nervously.

I don't say anything, I take her hand and lead her into my room. I close the door behind us and turn to her.

"Wes, what's going on?" She asks.

"First off, I'm sorry I acted like a prick last night. Second, we are staying here for a while. There's a lockdown. War with the Cartel is beginning. They followed me in your car today. Rip and the brothers dealt with them. It's not safe so all of the brothers and their families will come and stay here until things are safe again." I state, pulling her in my arms. I need to feel her, to smell her.

"What?" She whispers, fear and confusion in her eyes.

"I'm sorry but I can't tell you anymore. I can only tell you that I'm going with Rip now to meet with someone who can hopefully help the club. We need allies and if he agrees he will be a huge help." I stroke her cheek.

I lean in and kiss her softly. I sweep my tongue across hers, caressing and teasing her. I slow the kiss and rest my head against hers.

"It will all be okay, I promise." I whisper across her lips. "I have to go now but I will be back soon. Go sit with Rose. Patty and Raven will take care of you. I love you." I state.

"Love you too." She replies, her voice wavering slightly. She's clearly scared and worried. I hate that I can't be there for her right now and that I have to leave her, but I need to speak to Dreads. I need to make sure that he can help us, fight with us.

I leave her with the others. They embrace her in their arms and reassure me that she will be fine. I search for Rip and find him by the truck.

"Khan let's go." Rip orders.

Khan drives us to Dreads'. I've heard about this place but never seen it. It's a huge old plantation house surrounded by acres of land.

"Holy shit this place is huge." I mutter.

"Yeah. He's done well for himself that's for sure." Khan mutters.

We park up and I notice that there are men dotted all around the place carrying riffles, machine guns, and I think I see a guy carrying a damn rocket launcher.

Tank, Patty's friend and also Dreads' cousin, greets us at the door.

"Good to see you again Rip. Dreads is waiting for you." He states, leading the way.

We follow him to the outside decking where Dreads is sitting. He is sipping iced tea and wearing a navy designer suit, designer shoes, and shirt. He screams money. He stands and

I immediately understand why people respect him. He has a demeanour that requires, no, demands respect. I heard he bought this place because it's where his grandparents were enslaved. It had always been owned by white racist pricks and they must be turning in their graves that a powerful man, a grandson of slaves, now owns it. It's the ultimate fuck you, pure brilliance.

He shakes our hands.

"Sit please." He gestures.

We sit.

"Listen Dreads, I'm going to cut through the bullshit, we need your help. It's about the Cartel, it's Jesús. He's unpredictable and it's only a matter of time before he attacks. I lost a man to him before and I won't fuckin' lose another." Rip states.

Dread nods.

"What help do you need and why should I get myself involved in your mess?" He asks.

Rip goes to speak but I lean forward, interrupting him.

"Because it will be in your best interest. The Cartel get control over this town, this state, that's your business gone. What makes you think that once he's taken us out he would leave you alone and cut you a deal? He wouldn't. He's a sick son of a bitch and you know it. In any business deal he is a liability." I argue.

"I'm a smart businessman and any opposition that I have come up against, I have extinguished. Do not underestimate me Mr Stone, I will not be coerced or bullied into making a decision." He threatens.

"How do you know who I am?" I ask.

"As I said, do not underestimate me." He repeats.

"Fuck this, I'm out of here." I stand.

"Love. Love is what messes up business. It is most probably what causes most of the wars. Am I right?" Dreads asks.

I don't respond. He smirks and nods his head.

"Very well, I shall help you. I will get the intel and when the time comes we will have your back. It's easier to extinguish them sooner rather than later or I could have an infestation on my hands."

"You were going to help us anyway, weren't you?" I state.

He smiles and nods.

"Yes, of course. I like you guys. You're good people and Jesús is not. He is a cockroach that needs to be exterminated."

"Thanks Dreads, it's appreciated. I will be

in touch."

We stand as does Dreads and he shakes our hands. He stops at me and smiles.

"She must be very special."

"She is."

CHAPTER EIGHTEEN

Serena

Everyone is trying so hard to reassure me. They keep telling me it's fine, it's nothing. They keep saying that it will be okay but I know it won't be. This is partly because of me, because Wes and I are together.

Every time the door opens I turn and look for Wes. I need him right now. All I want is for him to hold me.

"They will be back soon." Patty leans over and tells me.

I give her a small smile.

"Listen, speaking as someone who has lived the biker life her whole entire life, it will all work out in the end. There may be some scary times but this crazy and scary family will always make sure you are okay. They will always make things right. I know you may feel shit scared right now but soon it will feel like a distant memory." Patty states and squeezes my hand reassuringly.

The door swings open and Rip, Khan, and Wes walk in. Rose runs up to Rip and jumps on him, wrapping her arms and legs around him and kissing him passionately.

Wes strides purposefully to me and pulls me to him and kisses me.

"Man where's my fucking greeting? What's a guy got to do to get some of that action?" Khan complains.

"Angel." He whispers across my lips.

Having him here and hearing him call me that calms me. I feel safe again.

"Let's get out of here." He states, and leads me to an outside area surrounded by trees. Wes pulls me down onto his lap under one of the trees.

"You need to know that things may get scary, they may get fucked up, but I will always protect you. I will always keep the danger away from you." He says sincerely. He tucks my hair behind my ear.

"But what about you, will you be safe from danger?" I ask him, linking my fingers behind his neck and stroking my nails slowly up and down.

"Angel, I laugh in the face of danger. Ha-ha." He jokes and laughs.

"Wes, I'm serious." I press.

He doesn't answer. He leans in, brushing his lips with mine.

"Kiss me." He demands softly. I kiss him without hesitation.

We don't have long before Wes gets called to church, which I find out is a meeting. I find the family standing around in the kitchen preparing dinner.

"Oh hey Serena!" Daisy calls.

"Hi, um, anything I can do to help?" I ask.

"Sure. Can you make up this sauce for me? There's the ingredients." She points to the chopped tomatoes and vegetables.

"Marinara?" I ask.

She smiles and nods.

"Yup, how did you guess?" She asks.

"I'm Italian." I laugh.

"Oh crap, of course." Daisy apologises.

"Well I expect it to be the best sauce we've ever had if it is being made by a proper Italian. No pressure." Patty winks.

I laugh and start chopping and putting all of the ingredients in a pan. I search for more seasoning.

"Oh my god that smells amazing." Rose

moans, sniffing the pot.

"Right come on. Let's take this lot out, the men are hungry!" Penny yells.

We all carry a dish out and place it on a massive table. The guys come in and pat their stomachs in appreciation of the food.

"Best marinara sauce I've ever tasted." Rose yells across the table to me.

All of the others mumble their thanks and appreciation for my sauce. I laugh and shake my head, a little embarrassed.

"Where did you learn to cook like that Serena?" Raven asks.

"My mama taught me. This was the first sauce I made when I was eight years old. Food is a big part of Italian culture." I smile.

"Well your dear Mamma would be proud of what you can cook. This is the best sauce I've ever tasted." Raven compliments.

We all eat and chat. You wouldn't think that there was a dangerous threat to them or the club. They're all just being carefree, laughing and joking with each other. All expect for Wes; he looks like he has the weight of the world on his shoulders. I'm that weight, I'm the reason he's so worried.

I reach for his hand and give it a gentle squeeze. His gaze comes to mine. I lean forward and kiss him.

"Stop worrying. It will be okay, you said so yourself." I whisper across his lips.

He doesn't say anything, he just kisses me back softly.

"Ewww, why does everyone have to kiss all the time?" Caden, Rose's son, yells.

"It womantic, isn't it Mamma?" Maddie, Patience's daughter, beams.

I laugh as does Wes.

"Right, who is up for dessert?" Trudy yells.

"Me!" All the children yell.

"I thought so." She mutters and clears some plates.

"Let me help you." I stand.

I help Trudy and Raven collect the plates and take out the trash.

"Oh I forgot to take this bag out, would you mind grabbing it?" Trudy asks.

"No worries." I state.

I go to the big wheelie bin and I think I see something. I stare for a moment, not sure what it was. There is nothing there. I shake my head. Must have been a racoon or something. I throw the trash in and head back inside.

I walk back into the kitchen and Raven and

Trudy are unloading the pies from the fridge.

"Let me help you." I state, taking a couple of pies.

"Hhmm these look go…" I don't finish my sentence.

A loud explosion and an unbelievably strong force has me hurtling forward, slamming me into the far wall. I hit my head and immediately black out.

CHAPTER NINETEEN

Wes

We were talking and laughing when the explosion happened. The kids screamed, scared, and the room filled with dust from the debris. When most people hear an explosion you run away from it to safety, but not me. I ran straight towards it. Serena.

"Everyone outside now!" Rip yells his orders.

"Serena!" I yell, coughing and squinting to see where I'm going through the dust cloud.

"Trudy! Raven!" I yell.

Silence. In that moment silence was the scariest fuckin' thing in the world. As I made my way forward to the door I prayed for a whimper, a cry, anything. I push on the door and it doesn't move. There's something blocking it. I push harder and harder.

"God damn it!" I roar angrily.

I turn back around and run to the back of the building.

"Wes, Wait." Big Papa and my uncle Max yell.

I don't wait for them to catch up. I hear footsteps behind me as I reach the back entrance to the kitchen. The door, the wall, and the window are gone; in their place is rubble.

"Fuck!" I yell, panicked. I grip my hair and move forward, lifting and moving slabs of brick and concrete.

The rest of the brothers come to help me. My back screams in agony from the weight I'm lifting but I don't care. I don't stop. I make a small gap and climb straight through.

"Wait Wes! Fuck!" Rubble yells.

I don't care, I need to get to her. The room is dark and I cough from the dust that's thick in the air.

"Serena! Trudy! Raven!" I yell.

I hear a groan to the right. I move quickly and find Trudy moving slowly, holding her head.

"Trudy, thank fuck. You okay? Can you stand?" I ask.

"Yeah, I think so." She groans in pain as I help her up.

"What the fuck happened?" She asks.

"Not sure. Come on, we need to get you out of here." I rasp. The thick dense air is starting to effect my lungs.

"Climb through there." I point, leading her to the small gap.

"Trudy is coming through!" I yell back to the guys.

I help to ease her through the gap. I turn back around and search for Serena and Raven.

"Over here!" Is coughed out.

I find Raven; her foot is trapped under the unit.

"Shit. Okay, if I can lift this can you move your leg out?" I ask.

"Yeah." She nods, panicked.

"Okay on three. One, two, three." I grunt as I manage to lift the heavy unit just enough for her to move her foot.

"I'm out." She breathes a sigh of relief.

I drop the unit back down. I reach for Raven and help her to her feet.

"Ahhh shit!" she cries in pain.

"Put your arm around me and I will help you. Your foot is probably broken." I say, placing her arm over my shoulders. She hops to the small gap.

"How the fuck am I going to climb through that with my broken foot?" She asks.

"I will lift you and the guys will have to pull you through from the other side." I say, climbing up a little bit of the rubble.

I lift Raven and she starts pulling herself through a little.

"Grab her hands! Pull her through!" I yell.

Soon they are pulling Raven through and I immediately carry on looking for Serena. I notice her boot and run straight to her.

"Angel." I call as I move part of units and cupboard doors that are laying on top of her.

She's unconscious and there's blood coming from her head. Pure fear runs through my veins.

"Shit. Wake up!" I say as I stroke her face.

She groans and moves slightly. I sigh in relief.

"It's okay, I'm going to get you out of here." I say as I reach down and pick her up.

I reach the small gap and wonder how I'm going to do this. I need help.

"I need someone to reach inside and grab Serena and pull her through. She's unconscious." I yell.

I hear mumbled voices and then Rubble

appears through the gap. He leans his top half through and holds out his arms to take her.

"Shit." He grits, seeing her bleeding head.

He carefully hooks under her arms and backs out as I feed the rest of her body through the gap. As soon as her feet are through I climb through, needing to hold her, needing to be with her.

Once back outside I take deep breaths to fill my lungs with fresh air. They had pulled Serena over to the side and Rose is lent over her. I go straight to her and take her hand in mine. Rose lifts her eyelids and shines her torch, looking into her eyes.

"Is she gonna be okay?" I rasp.

Rose nods.

"Yeah, she will be. She has a got slight concussion from her head injury." Rose states. "Here, apply pressure to the wound while I get the bandages from my bag." She shoves some gauze in my hand and leaves to grab her bag.

I place the gauze on her head and press gently. She moans. "Angel, it's me. You're gonna be okay. I've got you." I whisper on her lips before placing a gentle kiss.

Rose comes back and wraps her head with the bandage. It's a sea of chaos and panic, everyone is running about, children are crying, women are crying. It's like a war zone. Raven is taken straight to hospital for her broken foot but luckily Trudy only has a few cuts and bruises.

I sit there with Serena, blocking out everything. She is the only thing I care about. I just want her to open her eyes.

"Wes." Rose calls. I look up at her.

"You okay? I've called your name like five times." She asks, clearly concerned.

"I'm good, what is it?" I ask and clear my throat.

"We need to move her now. Can you pick her up or do I need to get some of the guys to help?" She asks.

"No, I've got her." I pick her up.

We carry her around to one of the trucks and I lay her on the back seat. I walk around the opposite side and carefully lift her head up onto my lap. I don't ask where we are going. I just sit in the back with Serena's head resting on my lap, stroking her cheek. Her eyes flutter open and she frowns. My heart feels like it's about to burst through my chest.

"What's going on?" She mumbles.

"Shhhh angel, rest. We are going somewhere safe." I whisper.

She hums and leans into my hands, falling

back unconscious.

Once we arrive Rip opens the truck door.

"You good? She good?" He asks.

"She will be, and I will be when she is. Where are we?" I ask.

He sighs.

"Let's get her settled inside and then I'm calling a meeting." He states, squeezing my shoulder.

I nod and he helps me get Serena out of the car. I follow him to a room where I lay her in bed and tuck her in. Rose comes in with Caden.

"Go. Go to the meeting. I will be checking her and making sure she's okay. I have my little helper here too. Isn't that right Dr Caden?" Rose smiles and winks at him.

"Yep. I've seen it all before in the movies. I totally know what I'm doing." He says confidently.

I look hesitantly to Rose.

"It's fine, go." She orders. She acts fearless but I can see the worry in her eyes.

I lean in and kiss her cheek.

"Thank you." I say quietly.

She nods and gives me an emotional smile.

I turn and leave, walking with Rip down

the large staircase. Everyone is moving about, going in and out.

"This is the only time I will allow you to kiss my wife." Rip states.

"She's struggling to hold it together." I point out.

"Yeah, I know. She won't break until Caden is out of sight. She's a fuckin' rock."

We walk along a long corridor and through many doors.

"How is Caden?" I ask.

"He's good. He sees his ma handling it well, helping, and he copies her. She will sit and have a long chat with him later. Now let's get this meeting over with cause I damn well know you're eager to get back to Serena and the brothers are wanting to be with their families right now." He says, opening a door to a large room where all of the brothers are waiting. They are anxious and agitated and rightly so.

"Brothers, listen up. I know we don't have the evidence but everything is pointing to the Cartel. Now while, like you, I am thirsty for blood, we need to sit and wait before making a move. Don't be disheartened because we will be making our move and we will be fuckin' killing them all!" Rip yells.

The brothers grunt and some of them

cheer.

"Y'all want to know where you are? It's an old farm and barn. I had it converted and the two buildings connected. There are twenty bedrooms and more than enough living space. It was kept for extreme emergency. None of you knew about it. It's off the books, it's completely off of the radar. If I had thought for even a second that the Cartel would come blowing up our motherfucking club I would have moved us here sooner." Rip states, lighting his cigarette.

"Now once things have settled, I'm calling Dreads. We are getting this shit sorted. It ends fuckin' now. I will not lose anyone else, I will not have anyone else get hurt. No one survives. We kill them all. We show them no mercy. Mess with the Satan's Outlaws and you will pay the motherfuckin' price!" Rip yells, angrily slamming his fist down onto the table.

"We have enough supplies here to keep us going for one month. I will be telling Dreads that is our deadline. In one month we will strike. No one is to leave this place, no one is to be seen outside of this land. If I catch you leaving then you're out of this club. We are a family. If one person leaves then they put us all at risk. I will not have any selfish cunts in my club." Rip threatens.

"I have one request." I declare. All heads

turn to me.

"Jesús is mine." I state.

Rip pauses for a second before nodding.

"Fine."

I'm the first to leave and head back upstairs to Serena. When I walk into the room she's awake and sipping water. I walk with purposeful strides. She puts down her glass and I take hold of her face and kiss her. I kiss her like I haven't seen her in a year. I kiss her with all of the emotion I have at the thought of losing her.

"Err, Caden and I will leave you too it now." I hear Rose scuttle away.

"Mum, I didn't know you could do that with your tongue. Is that why they call it tonsil tennis?" Caden asks.

"Shut up Caden." Rose mutters.

I laugh and break our kiss.

"That kid."

"He sure has a way with words." Serena smiles.

I sit on the bed beside her and stroke her cheek.

"How are you feeling?" I ask.

"Like I've been hit in the head with a sledgehammer." She snorts and winces.

I clench my jaw, hating the thought of her being in any pain.

"I'm going to fuckin' kill them." I growl.

She shakes her head.

"No, don't. Do not make yourself like them. Do not become one of them. They will pay for what they've done. The guilt will eat them up." She states.

I smile and climb on the bed, pulling her to me.

"I love that you have a kind heart. I love that you think people like this have a conscience. They don't. They don't give a shit about hurting people, it's what they do. There is no higher power that'll deal with them. We are the higher power, and we deal with them. I will deal with them. They cannot come and hurt you and my family. If you had died I would have hunted them down and killed them already, but you're alive. I won't hunt them down but when I meet them again I will fuckin' kill them." I confess.

To my surprise she doesn't flinch away at my statement, instead she looks up at me.

"Kiss me." She whispers.

CHAPTER TWENTY

Serena

I had a dreadful feeling in my gut after Wes confessed that he would kill the men that blew up the club. Something didn't sit right with me. It wasn't that I was scared at his statement or that it surprised me, I expected it. I expect that he will kill the men responsible. It's more, well, it's like the end of the world is coming. I just can't shake the feeling that there is this ticking time bomb that is about to go off and I have no idea how to defuse it.

I lay on a blanket staring up at the blue sky. The children are running around and playing on a makeshift swing made by Wes, Rip, Blake, and Carter on the tree by the lake. The kids want to swing and jump off of it. Well Caden does and Maddie and Miguel are just following him since he's the oldest.

"Maddie come and put your floaties on!" Patty yells from next to me. I sit up and smile.

"But Mamma I'm a big girl now so I don't need them!" Maddie stomps angrily to her mom.

I fight my laughter. She stands there in her cute little bathing suit with her hand on her hip, giving her mom attitude.

"Maddie, don't you get sassy with me. Put your floaties on." Patty reaffirms.

"But Mamma." Maddie protests.

"Princess, do as your mamma has asked." Axel backs Patty up.

"Okay." She huffs, holding out her arms for her mom to put on her floaties.

Once they're on she runs back to the swing.

"I swear that girl and her sass will be the death of me." Patty sighs.

"Yeah, fuck knows where she gets it from." Axel says sarcastically. Patty throws an apple at him as he jumps up. He laughs and runs off to the guys.

"Yeah you better run, pussy!" She yells after him.

"Patty, you've been a part of the Satan's Outlaws your entire life. Can I ask your advice on something?" I ask.

"Sure." She sits up and faces me.

"This war...I don't know...this whole thing. I'm not sure how I feel about it or if I'm scared for myself. I'm definitely scared for Wes and the guys. Will they really kill them? If our men will kill the Cartel, no questions asked, then surely the Cartel will kill them? God I'm rambling, of course they would, it's a war. Stupid Serena." I groan and shake my head.

"Don't. You're not stupid for asking those questions or feeling like you do. We all feel the same. We all want payback for what they did but we also want to keep our men safe. Look, the way you need to look at it is if the Cartel walked in here right now, they would kill us straight away without question." Patty states.

"What, even the children?" I ask.

"Sure, they would get caught in the crossfire. Now please don't get upset with me saying this but Jesús held me hostage and he ran my truck off of the road. Maddie was with me. You feel this desire not to harm others or think that deep down they give a shit about us, but they don't. The truth is, they don't, and if I could get my hands on your brother I'd kill him myself. Not for what he put me through but for what he did to Maddie." She states firmly.

"I get it, I do. I just, I don't know, this whole thing is new to me and it's a completely different situation to anything I've experienced. I never thought my life would be at risk like this and I never thought it would be my biological brother behind it. It's just so...so..."

"Fucked up?" Patty interrupts.

"Yeah, yeah, you could say that." I laugh.

Patty reaches over and squeezes my hand.

"Listen, no matter what is going on with the club, you can talk to me or anyone else. We are a family and we look out for each other. It takes some getting used to, believe me, and sometimes it will drive you insane, but through it all they are the one thing that's constant. They will always stand by your side."

I smile.

"Thanks. That's good to know. Sometimes I think Wes has enough on his plate to deal with without me adding my own personal worries to it."

We hear a scream and look over to see Caden flying through the air and splashing into the lake. He surfaces and cheers at the top of his lungs.

"That was awesome!"

Maddie is too scared to go so Axel strips down to just his jeans and sits on the swing with her. Her little arms hold on tight around his neck and they fly into the air and splash into the lake. I smile when Maddie yells excitedly.

"Again, again!"

Wes walks towards me and sits behind me, pulling me onto his lap.

"You going to jump in then angel?" He asks, nipping at my neck.

"Uhh I don't have my bikini so that would be a no. I think I will leave it to the kids." I reply.

"I would be more than happy for you to go skinny dipping." He retorts.

"Oh okay so shall I just strip off for all to see?" I ask, raising my eyebrow in question.

"Um fuck no. I meant just us. No way am I letting any other fucker see you naked." He grunts.

"That's what I thought." I laugh.

I lean back against him. There may be scary times looming over us but at this moment they are worth it. These carefree moments are what I will always cherish.

****

The next week is fun. We have massive cookouts and everyone is happy and laughing. We've been here for three weeks and there's no word on when we will be going back to normality. No word of what's coming next. I know the guys and I know that something is looming because as each day passes, the atmosphere changes. The air is filling with more tension and the brothers are exchanging looks they think we don't notice.

It's the middle of the night and I stir and wake up. Wes' side of the bed is empty. I rub my eyes and sit up. I see him staring out of the window.

"What's wrong?" I ask.

He spins around, snapping out of his daze. He gives me a small smile that doesn't reach his eyes.

"Nothing. I just can't sleep is all."

I peel back the covers and pat the bed.

"Come to bed." I whisper.

He walks back to bed and as soon as he is laid down I move to him. I climb on top of him and kiss him. I grind myself down on him, making him groan deep in his throat.

"Angel." He moans.

"Shh, just relax. I'm going to make you forget, even if it's just for a while." I whisper.

I take hold of his cock and slowly slide down, feeling him fill me inch by delicious inch. I pause for a moment to feel him inside of me, to feel him letting me be in control. His eyes are hooded, watching and waiting for me to move.

I rock slightly, making us moan. His hands graze my thighs and grip my hips. I rock and circle my hips, raising myself up and down his hard length. His lips part as I pick up the pace and his grip tightens. I move my hands over my body as I ride him, cupping my breasts and moaning. He moves his thumb across my clit, sending bolts of pleasure to my core.

"Oh God yes!" I cry.

He moves his hips up, thrusting in me as I ride him. My orgasm is building and my legs begin to shake.

"Wes! Fuck!" I cry as it hits me. I throw my head back and arch my back, the pleasure too much.

"Fuck!" Wes roars as he climaxes, slamming himself up into me.

I lean forward to kiss him whilst slowly rocking my hips.

"Better?" I ask against his neck as I kiss him.

"Yeah angel. I think need a little more though." He says and he flips me onto my back.

CHAPTER TWENTY-ONE

Wes

I know Serena can sense it, I know all of the women can. The tension is thick. All of us are going into battle not knowing what is waiting for us. We don't know whether we will all make it back out alive. It's worse not knowing, waiting. We all just want to get it over with now, whatever our fate may be.

I walk into Rip's office. Blake, Carter, and Axel are standing around.

"What's this all about?" I ask, looking at each of them.

"I've been speaking to Dreads and he was thinking that it may be a good idea to send Serena to meet with Jesús first. Maybe we can lure him into a false sense of security. We would also be able to get an idea of what we are walking into." Rip informs me.

"No fucking way." I grit.

"Wes, just listen. She would be safe.."

"Would you let fuckin' Lily go in there?!" I snap, interrupting Blake. He doesn't answer.

"No, I thought not. You wouldn't risk your own wives so why risk her?!" You can all go fuck yourselves!" I yell.

I turn to leave.

"He wants to meet her." Rip says. I pause at the door and turn back around.

"What?" I ask, frowning.

"He passed on a message to one of Dreads' men. He wants to meet his sister." Rip states.

I sigh and pinch my nose.

"Over my dead body." I state. "I am not having that psychopath near Serena! I don't give a flying fuck if it's her brother or not, he is not going near her." I refuse.

They all exchange a look.

"She said she will meet him." Axel states.

"You asked her?" I pace around the room. "You fuckin' asked her behind my back knowing full well she would do it if she thought it would help. You son of a bitch!" I yell and swing, hitting Rip right across the jaw. Blake, Carter, and Axel move quickly to hold me back.

Rip wipes the blood from his mouth with the back of his hand.

"Be angry at me all you want but if you were in my situation you would have done the same. I wouldn't put her life on the line if I thought he would actually do something to hurt her. You need to see it from my perspective. I have my men willing to go into this war fighting blind. Anything that may help them, anything at all that would mean keeping them safe, I have to do it. I have to protect my club." Rip points out.

I sigh.

"I knew this would fuckin' happen. I should never have introduced y'all to her. I should have kept her out of it, kept her safe." I sigh.

Rip hands me a bottle of whiskey. I snatch it and take a long swig. He rests his hand on my shoulder.

"She wants to do this, she wants to do her bit to help. I think she also wants to meet her brother. She's a strong woman that can handle her own. Believe me when I say that I wouldn't put her life at risk. I know you, I know you want to protect everyone, save everyone, but sometimes you will need help. Sometimes it's your woman who can help you." Rip states.

"He's right." Carter adds. "Look at Daisy, look how she managed to overcome what she went through. You need to let go, man. You can't control everything and stop every bad thing."

I don't say anything. I down more whiskey, letting it burn my throat.

"Wes, look at me." Blake states. "This isn't Ma. This isn't something you can control or prevent. Shit happens and no matter how much you may try to shield her, you can't. The only thing you can do is be by her side and protect her, be ready to defend her when she needs you."

"I still don't like putting her in harm's way in front of that fuckin' psycho. If she goes, I go. That's the bottom line. I will not send her in alone." I relent.

They all look to Rip and wait for his response. His ice cold gaze is fixed on me.

"I'm not backing down. That's the only way I will let her go." I affirm.

Rip's jaw tenses and then he nods.

"Fine, but I don't fuckin' like it. I honestly don't think he would hurt her, but he will have no problem hurting you. Be careful and don't get yourself killed. We will drive you there and pick you up." He states.

"No, they won't allow it. It has to be us and us alone. The Cartel will escort us when we are near his place. I've seen them do it. You need to stay back and keep hidden." I warn them.

"Fuck. I don't like this. I don't have a good

feeling about this." Axel states.

"None of us have a good feeling about this but we don't have a lot of choice. We need to figure out a way in and at the moment that's our only way. He wants to meet Serena." Rip points out.

I stand and walk to the door. I pause and turn around to face them.

"It will be fine. I've been watching them for months. I know how they work. It's safer for me to be in there than any of you. Just make sure when all this is over we have one big fuckin' party." I smile and wink.

I walk into the bedroom and see Serena reading on the bed. Her eyes come to me and she puts down her book and turns to me.

"They told you what's happening." She states, not questioning. She knows just from the look on my face.

"Yeah. Tell me, when were you going to tell me? Or were you just going to give me the slip and have me panicking for hours?" I ask, trying my best to keep the anger out of my voice.

"I knew you would be mad. I knew you wouldn't understand. Rip asked me. He didn't pressure me and said I wouldn't have to do it if I didn't want to. I want to meet my brother. I want to see if maybe...maybe I can get through to him. Did you ever think of that? That maybe I could get through to him? He may be a monster, he may have killed, but so have you, so have all of the brothers. I need answers. I need to know him and know what my father was like." Serena argues.

I sigh, gripping my hair, and look up.

"I get it, I do. That's why I'm coming with you. I'm telling you now, do not expect a nice family reunion because it won't be, you won't change his mind." I warn her. I tuck her hair behind her ear and stroke her cheek.

"It's not safe for you to come with me. What if they hurt you?" She asks with worry in her eyes.

I smile and kiss her forehead softly.

"They won't kill me because I'll have you protecting me. Plus if they try it I will kill them first." I wink.

She grips my shirt and rests her face in the crook of my neck.

"I will protect you just like you protect me." She whispers.

The next morning we wait for the call to say it's time to go. I know Serena is on edge. She's nervous and is trying to do anything she can to keep herself busy.

I sit out the back and watch the kids run around carefree. They're playing chase, screaming, and laughing.

"Ah what I wouldn't give to be that young and oblivious to it all." I hear Uncle Max say.

I turn and smile at him as he wheels himself next to me. He is a constant reminder that war can go wrong. Well, him and both of my parents being dead.

"You know you've always been the warrior, the one that was going to protect us all and make sure nothing bad would happen to us. What is it you used to always say to me as a kid?" Max pauses and smiles. "Ah yeah, that was it, *'don't worry uncle max I will always protect the family. It's my duty.'* I should have told you at that point that it wasn't your job or your duty. You were just a kid but with what you had been through, I figured it gave you a purpose. When I praised you for keeping us safe you would beam with pride. What I'm trying to say is, and failing badly, is that not once was it ever your duty to protect your family. It should have been your pa and it should have been your ma too. You were just a kid, you missed out on all of this." Max gestures to the kids.

"It was what it was. We can't go changing that now. Pa was a shit father and an even shittier husband. Ma should have left his ass long before then. She failed as a ma the moment she didn't leave and kept us in that house with him.

You've got to remember that Blake had it worse than me and for longer. At least I got some of my childhood back. Oh and there's Maggie, she managed to get away from it altogether." I state.

"Hhmm, that she did. Would be nice for her to have stayed in contact though. Listen boy, I ain't about to give you my life's fuckin' wisdom because, well, I ain't got that much. I just want to say that I've always been proud of you boys. I've always loved you like you're my own. When this is all done with, enjoy your life. Don't try and protect everyone and everything. Enjoy every moment you have with your woman. Now I'm off to get myself a beer. Would you smile? You're an ugly fucker when you don't." He teases.

"Fuck off Max." I laugh.

I hear a whistle and I turn and see Rip. He lifts his chin to call me over.

"What is it?" I ask when I reach him.

"It's time." He states.

"Fine. I will get Serena. Meet you out front in ten." I reply, walking back to the house.

CHAPTER TWENTY-TWO

Serena

We sit in silence on the way to the Cartel's house. Well, I guess I should say my brother's house. I'm trying to calm my nerves, trying to show Wes that I'm not scared. He reaches across, takes my hand, and places a soft kiss on my palm.

"It will be okay." He reassures.

"I know, I'm fine." I smile.

Wes raises his eyebrow in question, seeing through my bullshit.

"Sure you are." He smirks and shakes his head.

"Well here we go." He mutters, looking in his rear view mirror as a black SUV follows us.

"Oh shit." I whisper.

Wes squeezes my hand and I take a deep breath. I feel like my heart is beating a million times per second. It's like those movies where they send in a mole and they are wired up, trying to record vital bits of evidence.

Suddenly another open back truck pulls in front of us with two guys on the back. They're aiming their guns at us. One of them signals for us to follow. We are now completely surrounded by them.

"Oh my god. How have they got guns like that on display in broad daylight?" I panic.

"Angel, this is the Cartel, the law doesn't apply to them. No cops will even dare interfere with them. I bet half of them are paid off anyway." Wes grits through his teeth, gripping the steering wheel.

We turn into a huge gated driveway. Up ahead is huge house, it is a borderline mansion.

We stop and Wes turns to me and pulls me in. I kiss him briefly.

"No matter what happens, you get yourself out of here. Don't worry about me, only worry about yourself."

I look around as men with guns start to surround our truck.

"Wes, I'm not going to leave you. I…"

"Just promise me." He interrupts and cups my face. I swallow nervously and nod.

He gives me a small smile.

"Good. Let's get this over with." He breathes before kissing me and jumping out of the truck. He holds his hands behind his head.

They yell at him in Spanish and aim their guns. Wes gets on his knees. I'm shaking and praying that they don't hurt him. My truck door is wrenched open and I'm dragged out. I scream. Wes looks to me calmly and shakes his head in warning. I stop screaming and try to calm myself down and do what they want. The large front door opens and out steps a handsome looking guy in a white shirt and black tailored suit trousers. He's rolling his shirt sleeves up. He looks around at the commotion and frowns. His eyes land on me and he smiles.

"Mi hermana, mi hermosa hermana." He beams, opening his arms wide.

He notices that his guard has got my hands behind my back and is gripping my hair tight. He walks past one of his guards and takes his gun. Without warning he shoots the guard that's restraining me. Blood splatters across my face. I scream. I'm terrified. He chucks the gun back to his guard and brushes his hands together like he has just taken out the trash. He smiles again.

"Mi hermana, my apologies for the less than welcome reception." He apologises and pulls me into his arms. My whole body is shaking from shock and fear.

He frowns and pulls back a little and tuts.

"Oh I'm sorry. Let's get you cleaned up. We have so much catching up to do." He states. Taking my arm he starts to escort me to the house.

His men drag Wes, catching Jesús attention. He turns his face and transforms from the warm smiling welcome I got to a thunderous cold murder.

"Who the fuck is that?!" He roars, making me jump.

"Err, that's my boyfriend Wes. He drove me here to meet you. I love him, please don't hurt him." I rush out.

He clucks his tongue and throws his head back laughing.

"Wes!" He clicks his fingers and taps his head. "Si, Wes Stone. Ahh your brother is Blake and your cousin is the infamous Rip. Shame hermana, I thought you may have had better taste. Still!" He claps. "Today shall not be ruined, no? Please follow me and…err…Wes, I suppose you must come too."

He places his hand on my back and guides me through his house straight to the back patio where maids and waiters are waiting with drinks. The table is all set for dinner.

"¡Sorpresa! No expense spared. I have the finest food from around the world just for us.

Serena, mi hermana, I have had the best Italian chefs prepare food just for you!" He claps, smiling wide.

"Thank you." I say quietly.

"Sit, Wes. I did not know you were coming so I did not set a place for you and, well, it's rude to show up uninvited. At the very least you should notify the host, so if you don't mind, you can take a seat over there." Jesús states.

I look at Wes as he is shoved to the chair further along the patio. Jesús coughs, bringing my attention back to him. He holds out a chair for me and I smile and sit down.

He takes his seat and clicks his fingers. Staff pour our drinks and place our food down.

"Eat, please eat. I am not religious. I do not say grace." He smiles and takes a bite out of his prawn. I smile nervously and start to eat, taking small bites. My stomach is in knots and I'm so nervous that I'm struggling to eat.

"¡Parada!" Jesús yells, making me jump.

"What is it? What is wrong? Is the food not to your liking?" He asks. Before I can answer he has a gun pointed at the chef.

"No, no stop. Please, the food is delicious. It's just that, well, I'm so nervous about meeting you that I don't think I can eat." I smile anxiously.

He pauses and smiles and nods.

"Si, you're right. How stupid of me! Clear this food away now and all of you fuck off. Leave me and mi hermana alone. We have years to be catching up on." He clicks his fingers and the staff scurry away like little ants.

Pulling the chair beside me he sits down.

"Tell me. Tell me about your childhood, tell me about your madre." He asks.

As I sit he hands me a fresh cloth to wipe my face. My hands shake as I wipe the blood remnants off of my face. I swallow back the bile that rises up my throat and nod.

"Okay well I had an okay childhood. My mamma was loving. She raised us by herself." I state.

"Us? Ah, forgive me." He clicks his fingers. "Your brother." He smiles.

I suck in a breath and nod. "Yes, but he and my Mamma they, um, well…"

"Died in a crash." He interrupts coldly.

"Yes." I whisper. I'm desperate to move on. "After they passed I found a box of photos and letters from my mamma to…err…our father. He talks about you in them." I smile.

His eyes have turned dark, so dark I would swear they are black.

"My padre, talking about me? I find that hard to believe. Our father was a cold man, a man without feeling or emotion. I relished the day he died."

I swallow nervously and clear my throat.

"I suppose it's a good thing I never met him then." I say, giving him a tight smile.

He reaches over and places his hand on mine. I flinch. "Do not be scared of me, mi hermana. I would never cause you harm. You, like me, are a product of an absent father. I also had an absent mother but at least you had yours. Probably why you have a warm heart and mine is cold and dead." He laughs.

Curiosity gets the better of me and a very small part of me feels sorry for him.

"Why? What happened to your mother? Did she pass away?" I ask.

He looks away and his jaw clenches. Clearly I've hit a nerve. His gaze returns to mine and I suck in shuddery breath at the pain in his eyes.

"Mi madre, she may as well have been dead. Our father married my mother but he never really loved her. He treated her like she was a piece of dirt on his shoe. She loved him, she breathed for him. She worshiped the ground he walked on. But it didn't fill the emptiness she felt, the constant rejection. She soon found a way to fill that void: prescription drugs and alcohol. She would blame me for mi padre not loving her. She said I was the reason he hated her and that he hated me. She said I was only good for taking over the business, that is all I was bred for, the only purpose of my life." He states.

Without thinking I squeeze his hand and his eyes flicker to mine. Briefly I see a glimmer of warmth in his eyes, but the moment is broken. There's a commotion and one of his men has Wes on the floor and kicks him in the stomach. I jump up and run to him.

"Stop! Stop! What are you doing? Leave him alone." I shout as I kneel down and cup Wes's face.

"What's going on?" Jesús asks angrily.

"He mouthed off and spat on my shoes so I kicked the shit out of him, boss." The guy shrugs.

"Ah well, there! You see, no harm. Come Serena, I want to show you my rose garden." Jesús smiles and holds out his hand, waiting for mine.

"No. I will not be leaving Wes. That was uncalled for and he hit and attacked Wes. Why in the hell would I come and look at your rose garden?" I snap.

"Angel, just go." Wes coughs, holding his stomach.

"No." I reply.

"I see we have a problem here, and that problem is him. All I wanted was a nice meeting with mi hermana, and now you've ruined it by making her worry about you." He states, pointing at Wes. He spins around to the guy that kicked Wes.

"And you ruined it by making her sad because you kicked him. You interrupted our reunion." He says.

He pulls his gun out and shoots him straight between the eyes. I jump and scream. I watch as his lifeless body falls to the floor.

"There, now the problem is solved. Come Serena, let me show you this rose garden." Jesús smiles.

"Go." Wes says again.

I nod and stand on shaky legs. He takes my hand and leads me to his Rose garden. I look back at Wes; his eyes are fixed on me. I mouth the words 'I love you'.

As we wander through the garden Jesús seems calmer and more relaxed.

"I know you like flowers. I've seen your shop. The business does well?" Jesús asks.

"Yeah, it does alright." I answer.

"Are you wondering how I knew about

you?" He asks.

I nod. It's the one question we have all been wondering.

"Well, you see, I had overheard my padre talking with his right hand man about house payments. He gave orders to store the details elsewhere so they could never be traced. I asked him what was it for. He lied of course, told me some made up shit. Anyway, after he died I tracked down his man and got the information from him. Easy." He shrugs. He stops, waiting for my response.

"Oh, um, well done." I praise. He smiles wider. That seems to have pleased him somewhat.

We walk back to the house and they appear to have cleared away the dead guy. Thank god. I can't walk fast enough to Wes, as soon as I reach him I kiss him.

"I want to go home." I whisper and Wes nods.

Wes was right, this meeting isn't anything like I expected. I thought maybe if I could speak to him and reason with him I could get him to change his mind. Clearly Jesús doesn't have a clear sound mind for me to reason with. He is beyond messed up.

I turn back around to face Jesús. He has a dark expression across his face.

"Um, I have to go now. I am so happy to have met you." I lie.

Jesús smiles.

"Of course. I don't want to keep you from your busy life. We will see you out to your car." He gestures and we follow him out.

"Give me the keys." I whisper to Wes.

He frowns.

"Why?" He asks, confused.

"Because I think they are less likely to follow us if I'm the one driving. We will go to my shop to be sure and we will wait there until we know it is safe." I whisper, taking the keys from his hand. I just want to get out of here.

CHAPTER TWENTY-THREE

Serena

Wes jumps into the passenger seat while I say my goodbyes to Jesús. I'm a little taken aback when he pulls me in for a tight hug. I wouldn't say I was surprised because in the few hours I've been in his presence he has killed two of his men. Wes was right, he is unpredictable. Jesús is full of bad surprises.

"Mi hermana, how I have longed for a sibling. You have my word that I shall always have your back and look out for you." He states passionately.

"Thank you. I…err…appreciate it." I stutter my reply, not really knowing how to respond to that.

"Forgive me mi hermana." He whispers in my ear.

"Whaa…" My voice dies in my throat as gunshots ring out. I spin around and see Jesús men firing at the truck. I scream and go to run to the truck, but Jesús wraps his arm around my waist, keeping me back. I claw and kick, disparate to get to Wes. I scream his name over and over. Only when they stop firing does he let me go. I run.

"Wes?!" I scream.

I open the truck door which is now full of bullet holes. My heart is beating erratically. It's like I'm seeing everything in slow motion. There, slumped forward, is Wes. He's not moving and there is blood everywhere.

My hand reaches out. I'm shaking.

"Please Wes, please wake up. I love you. You have to be okay. I need you. Please." I sob.

My hands are covered in blood as I try to move him so I can see his face. When I manage to move him I scream and jump back as if I've been burned. Staring back at me are his beautiful lifeless blue eyes.

"Noo! Noo!" I scream. My body shakes and I cup his face.

"No! I can't lose you. I can't." I cry. I try covering my hand over the wounds to stop the blood. There is too much and I can't stop the flow.

"Come on, please. God, please." I sob.

Jesús appears at the door. There's no remorse on his face.

"I'm sorry Mi hermana, but it was necessary. Tell Rip this is only the beginning. You will forgive me in time. Now drive." Jesús says before slamming the door shut. He walks away, not looking back.

My whole body is shaking and I can't see clearly from the constant tears falling. I start up the truck and put my foot down, the tyres screeching as I leave. I sob and cry. I swerve around other cars, driving fast. I look over to Wes' lifeless body and grip my heart in pain. I scream. I turn down the small dirt track road to the house and I don't slow down. I pull up, speeding in front of the house. The front door opens and Rip, Blake, and the others step out to see what all of the noise is about.

Shaking I open my door and jump out. Sobbing, I scream.

"They killed him! He's dead!" I cry and fall to my knees. I watch as Blake runs straight to the truck and opens Wes' door.

"No! Fuck no! Brother!" He yells. He reaches in and pulls him out, laying him on the ground. "Wes come on, you can't fuckin' die, do you hear me?" Blake yells and starts CPR.

I cry on my knees, rocking back and forth and watching on. I'm praying for a miracle, praying that he will somehow be okay. Mammoth tries to pull Blake off of him.

"Come on brother, he's gone. There's nothing you can do." Blake shrugs him off. "Fuck off. He can't die, he can't fuckin' die." He croaks, tears now streaming down his face.

Arms come around me to pick me up but I fight them. "No. I'm not leaving him. I'm never leaving him." I protest.

Blake continues for I don't know how long. Eventually he stops. He's panting and out of breath and his hands are covered in blood. He lets out a pained sob. Lily runs to him and cradles him in his arms.

They all stand around, women sobbing, brothers silent, as the realisation hits that he's gone.

Rose comes out with a blanket and lays it over Wes. The sun begins to set and the darkness takes hold, filling not just the sky but my heart. The tranquil nights are no more. Instead the cries of pain and despair fill the night sky.

****

It's the next morning. I sit, wrapped in a blanket on the porch swing, watching the sun rise. I've been here all night. Patty tried to get me to come inside to go to bed but I couldn't. I can't. If I close my eyes, even for a second, all I see is his dead lifeless eyes staring back at me.

I hear the door open and someone comes to sit next to me. I don't look, I don't move. I just keep looking straight out ahead to the fields.

"Here, drink this." I ignore them.

"Serena, you need to drink or eat." They repeat.

I still don't move or acknowledge them. They sigh and place the cup down but don't leave.

"You know it's my fault, I should have never asked you to go and meet with him. I knew in my gut. I knew as soon as he said that you could only go if he went with you. Fuck!" Rip fumes, his voice cracking with emotion.

I look at him, hunched forward with his elbows on his knees and his face in his hands.

"It's not your fault." I say quietly. His head lifts up and his ice blue eyes land on mine. The normal cold and hard eyes are now broken. All I see is a mirror of my own pain and sadness.

"It's my fault." I rasp.

Rip frowns.

"And how did you come to that conclusion?" He asks.

"Jesús is my brother. None of this would have happened if Wes had nothing to do with me. You wouldn't have asked me to meet with him. Wes went because of me. He went to try and protect me. When I should have protected him and refused to go! I should have protected him!" I sob.

Rip moves and pulls me into his arms, trying to comfort me.

"It's not your fault. He loved you. There isn't one of us in this damn club who wouldn't lay down our life for the woman we love. Don't go fuckin' blaming yourself." Rip states. I feel him pick me up. I'm cradled in his arms, sobbing. He lays me down in bed and I try to fight him to get up.

"No, I can't sleep. I can't. I see him, I see his lifeless eyes. I can't. Please." I beg.

I feel a sharp scratch in my thigh.

"Ow! What was that?" I ask. I turn to see Rose with a needle in her hand.

"It's to help you sleep honey." She says softly.

I feel fuzzy and warm and my eyes become heavy.

"Wes. I need W..." I mumble before I drift off into darkness.

CHAPTER TWENTY-FOUR

Serena

I stay in bed. I don't leave my room. Different people come in and out to bring me food but I barely touch any of it.

I'm not sure how many days it has been. I lay here, just staring out of the window.

I hear the door open but I don't move. I feel the bed dip as someone sits beside me.

"You know, people always thought Wes and I had a thing for each other. They thought that we were going to get together." Daisy states.

I look at her and she smiles a small sad smile.

"But it was never like that for us. Wes and I shared a connection, sure, but it was a friendship. We had both been controlled and helpless at one point in our lives and so we understood each other. He was always there for me when I needed him and he gave me a good talking to as well. He was always good at listening and giving a pep talk." She sniffs. She pauses to wipe away her fallen tears.

"I know it has only been five days so I'm not about to give you the whole 'you have to live your life speech'. The truth is, if I lost Carter I'm not sure how I would handle it. I'm here, that's all I wanted to say. Anytime." She squeezes my hand and then leaves.

The days continue much the same. Food is dropped in and I pick at it and lay back down. I don't speak to anyone, I don't say a word. I stay inside myself, inside my pain and misery.

It's raining outside. I watch as the raindrops fall down the window. I sit up and sniff my hair and scrunch up my nose in disgust. Not having showered or anything for however long it's been, I decide to go for a shower. I wash my hair and scrub at my body. Once I'm finished I put on my robe.

As I step out of the bathroom I become lightheaded. I can't stop myself. I fall, fainting, and hit the ground with a thud.

I wake to see Rose waving something under my nose that makes me cough.

"There you go." She says while helping me

to sit up.

"Here, drink this." She hands me a glass of orange juice and I drink it.

She helps me up and guides me back into bed. She perches herself next to me and smiles.

"So it's good that you've had a shower. To be honest you were stinking up the place a little bit." She jokes.

"You need to eat more. At the very least you need to make sure you drink sugary drinks if you're really not in the mood for eating. Your body needs something to keep it going." She advises with concern in her eyes.

"The funeral is in three days." She informs me. My eyes snap up to hers and I suck in sharp breath.

"What? Why? I'm not ready…I…"

Rose interrupts.

"It's been sixteen days honey, he needs to be put to rest. It's only fair."

"Sixteen days?" I ask.

She nods.

"Um, well I guess that's okay."

"Do you want to come down and eat with us tonight? It might do you good to be with family." She offers.

"Fine." I relent. Rose smiles and squeezes

my hand. She stands and opens my wardrobe and pulls out my plain blue maxi dress.

I put it on and it hangs off of me from all of the weight I've lost. Rose isn't quick enough to hide her shock at my weight loss. I haven't eaten a meal since before Wes. I can't bring myself to eat properly. Beneath it all I feel like I don't deserve to be the one alive. Wes should be here, not me.

"Come on. Let's get you some food." She holds out her hand like she's afraid I will change my mind and bolt.

I can hear the loud chattering of people and some laughter. We walk into the dining room and heads turn in our direction. I look down to the floor, avoiding their gaze.

I hear feet approach. I look up into a similar pair of blue eyes. Blake.

My eyes fill with tears. He pulls me to him and hugs me tight.

"It's not your fault." He whispers in my ear. I let out a little sob.

He pulls back and I wipe my tears.

"I'm so sorry." I whisper back.

I see him tense at my words. He fights back his emotion and nods.

He clears his throat.

"Come on. Let's get you fed, you're skin and bone. Wes would kick my ass if I didn't take care of you."

He wraps his arm around me and walks with me to the table. I sit down and give everyone a tight smile. I'm trying to avoid the look of pity and sadness that's in everyone's eyes.

We all eat. The mood is different than before, it's quieter. People are barely talking because of the pain we are all feeling. I eat some of my food. I'm not able to stomach a great deal.

Trudy comes and sits next to me. She takes my hand in hers and the pain in her eyes is too much to bare.

"Serena, you know you're family right? Just because…" She pauses, finding the strength. "Just because Wes isn't here anymore that doesn't mean you aren't family. We will always be here for you. You were so important to Wes." She sniffles. "So that means you are important to us. These are hard times and we all need to lean on one another. Don't be afraid to do that, okay?" She says. She wipes her fallen tears away.

I nod and smile through my own tears. She hugs me and kisses the top of my head before leaving me. I feel the most bizarre feeling; I feel warm and loved. At the same time, I feel broken. I feel so broken that I'm not sure I will ever be able to put myself back together in the same way

I was. To feel loved yet feel so empty, lonely, and dead inside is a surreal feeling.

****

It's the day of the funeral. Wes is to be buried in the grounds. It's for safety but also so he is always close to us.

I stand in front of the mirror and stare at myself in my plain black dress. I've lost so much weight that my clothes hang off of me. My collar bone is protruding and my eyes are sunken. I look gaunt. I feel weak. I'm constantly nauseous. I can't stomach too much food or I'm sick. I'm tired and drained. All of the things that were once good, all of the things that used to make me smile, are gone. I'm in a deep dark depression and I can't seem to find a way out.

There's a knock on the door which makes me jump. Lily sticks her head around the door.

"It's time." She says softly. I nod and follow her downstairs.

The house has probably around forty people in it but it's silent. Everyone is wearing black. The brothers are wearing black with the Satan's Outlaws kutte over the top. They are all parted, waiting for me to walk out of the door.

As I step outside I see his casket. My steps falter and I wobble a little. Lily and Rose come either side of me to help me. Trudy, Raven, and

Penny are behind us. I can hear them sobbing. Daisy and Patty join us as we walk down the steps.

Blake, Rip, Carter, Axel, Mammoth, Rubble, Khan, and Ben stand either side of the casket. They crouch and lift, placing it on their shoulders. Ahead of them in his wheelchair is Max who leads the precession.

We follow, walking to an outside area made up with chairs and a stand. A sob escapes me when I see the large photograph of Wes.

We take our seats as Rip stands with a bit of paper in his hand.

"This isn't something I ever thought I would have to do. If anything, I thought he would be burying me. He was always fixing my shit for me, well not just mine, everyone's." He pauses, swallowing a lump in his throat. "Wes was never an official member of the Satan's Outlaws, but he empowered the brotherhood more than most of us. He helped anyone he could. If you needed him, he was there. He would always have your back with no questions asked." He smiles.

"It appears that the fucker planned for this day." He states. My head snaps up at this admission.

"He wrote down exactly what he wanted and also wrote a letter to be read out, which

Blake will do in just a minute. He gave this note to my pa five years ago and told him to only open if he croaks. Of course, none of us expected it to actually happen." He clears his throat and pinches his nose. "But it did. Now we can celebrate his life and know we are doing it the way he wanted. So before Blake reads the note from Wes, he wanted some music to be played." Rip looks to the bit of paper and laughs. "His words: '*play stairway to heaven by Led Zeppelin, the full length version. I want you to mourn me bitches.*' So for you Wes, here's your wish." Rip says as he hits play.

There's small laughter and sobs as we listen to the song. I can't take my eyes off of the casket, off of Wes. Tears fall down my face and I don't wipe them away. My shoulders shake, racked with sobs. The pain I feel is too much.

This is goodbye. I didn't have long enough with him and now he's gone. I never expected to have to say goodbye to him, especially not like this.

As the song picks up and the guitar builds, Mammoth hoots.

"Yes Wes brother!" I can't help smiling and there are a few chuckles.

When the song finishes Blake stands up with a bit of paper gripped tight in his hand.

"Wes wrote this for me. I don't think he

wanted it to be read out, but I felt that it had to be." He pauses, taking a breath. "Blake, if you're reading this then I'm gone. Or Uncle Max is an asshole and has given it to you." Blake smiles. "Well I guess age before beauty doesn't mean shit huh? If I'm dead and you're reading this now. Just know this: I was the better looking brother. Do me a favour, don't get all down and shit. Celebrate me, celebrate life. Take my place in looking after everyone." Blake pauses, taking a deep breath before he continues reading.

"Find love if you haven't already and live your life. Don't be a miserable prick." Blake smirks and his gaze come to mine. "If, when I die, I have a woman, look after her. Getting over me isn't going to be easy. I'm pretty sure I rocked her world. Play this next song for her. Tell her I love her, and even though when writing this letter I don't know who she is, I know she is special. She will be my world. Tell her I'm sorry that we didn't get forever but I promise I will continue to haunt her so she never has to live without me." Blake smiles sadly. I'm uncontrollably sobbing now.

"I love you brother. Now go get blind drunk." Blake sniffs. He folds the piece of paper up and places it in his pocket. "This is for you Serena." He hits play and Kodaline's 'All I Want' plays out of the speakers.

I sit and listen to the words as they lower

his casket into the ground. Everyone each takes a turn to throw a rose. I don't get up, I just sit there. Only once everyone has gone do I get up and stand over his grave.

"I love you Wes. You've taken a piece of me with you that will only ever belong to you. I love you so much it hurts. God, I would give anything to have you here with me. I miss you so much." I state while rubbing my chest. The pain in my heart is too much for me to bare. I pick up a single white rose and I kiss it. I release it into the grave.

"Goodnight Wes." I sob. I slowly walk away, leaving behind my heart with the only man I've ever loved.

All of the brothers and family gather for drinks and continue the celebration of Wes' life well into the night. I keep conversation light and mainly keep to myself. I sit with a water outside in the quiet of the night, not feeling like drinking or being around anyone.

The moment is broken when voices approach. Lily, Daisy, Rose, and Patty come out with tequila and deck chairs. They all set up next to me, creating a circle.

Rose pours us all shots then hands one to each of us. I decline.

"No thanks. I'm not in the mood to be

drinking or for having company to be honest." I admit.

"Well, you're shit out of luck there because last time I checked you're a part of this family. When we see one of our own hurting, needing help, needing support, we are there for them. Right now you need a stiff drink and some family around you." She argues back, shoving the shot in my hand.

Lily stands.

"To Wes, the best brother-in-law a girl could ever have." She toasts and then downs the shot. The rest follow, downing their shots. They look at me and I reluctantly do the same. I cough as the alcohol burns my throat.

Patty stands as Rose refills our shots.

"To Wes, the kindest and most caring soul I've ever known." She downs her shot and we do the same.

Rose refills and stands.

"To Wes, the protector of my sisters." She toasts and we all down our shots.

Next Daisy stands up.

"To Wes, my dear friend, I will miss your words of comfort and your warm hugs." She rasps, fighting her emotions.

We all down our shots and their eyes come to me. Rose raises her eyebrow in question. I nod and hold out my glass. She smiles and fills it. I stand and hold my glass up high.

"To Wes, my protector, my best friend, my lover, my only love. I will miss the way you made me laugh, the way you made me feel so special. I will miss your kisses. I will forever miss everything about you, my world. I love you Wes." I sniff and down my shot.

The girls all stand with their shots high in the air.

"To Wes." They yell before downing their shots.

I wipe my eyes and smile.

"Thanks, I think I needed that. I'm going to take myself off to bed now. I will see you in the morning." I smile and turn to leave. I don't miss the exchange of looks between them, the constant concern everyone appears to have. I am grateful that they care but right now I need to shut out this day and be alone.

CHAPTER TWENTY-FIVE

Serena

I lay up in my room for three days, lacking the motivation to do anything or see anyone. On top of depression which I'm sure I'm suffering from, I feel ill. I feel like I'm constantly going to throw up and nothing seems to settle my stomach.

The door bursts open and in storm Rose, Lily, Daisy, and Patty.

"Intervention!" Lily yells.

I jolt upright and place my hand over my erratic heart.

"What the hell? You scared the shit out of me." I curse.

"Sorry but we've tried the nicey, nicey tactics and it hasn't worked. Now we are coming in full blown like a hurricane and we're going to sort you out." Rose states firmly.

"I appreciate it but I'm okay. I just need to be alone." I shrug and lay back down.

"Oh hell no. You have been alone now for nearly three weeks and look at the state of you!" Rose argues back.

"Err Rose, maybe not so brutal." Daisy mutters.

"Nope! She's getting full brutal honesty!" Rose states. She steps forward and sits next to me.

"Now listen, we know that losing Wes is the worst thing that could ever happen. We can't even imagine what you're going through right now. But honey, Wes wouldn't want this. You've lost at least thirty lbs since losing him. You're not eating and you look pale and gaunt. If you want to mourn him, then that's alright, you should. You need to grieve but don't kill yourself doing it. Wes wouldn't want you like this. So let us help you, let us make you feel just a little bit better." She shrugs, squeezing my hand.

I look to the others and they all give me a small smile. I roll my eyes and relent.

"Fine. So what are you all here to do? Give me a make-over?" I ask.

"Not exactly. Mother!" Daisy yells.

In walks Penny with a tray of food. She

smiles and places it down for me.

"Good old English beef stew and dumplings. There's sherry trifle for pudding. Food that warms the heart." She smiles.

I take a mouthful of the food and as soon as I do my stomach rolls. I clasp my hand over my mouth, jump from the bed, and run to the bathroom. I empty my stomach down the toilet.

"Mum! What the hell did you put into the stew?!" Lily asks, taking a bite.

"Nothing unusual I swear! Just the normal ingredients I always use." Penny defends.

I reach for the towel and wipe my mouth.

"It's not penny's fault. I've been feeling this way for a while. I can't seem to keep anything down at the moment." I breathe. Patty hands me a cup of water which I gratefully sip.

"Back in a minute." Rose says and then walks out of the room.

"Where is she off to?" Patty asks. They just shrug.

"Maybe you have a bug, you have been run down lately. You can pick up all sorts when you're not feeling yourself." Penny says as she strokes the hair from my face and places a damp cloth on my forehead. I smile at her motherly attentiveness.

They help me up. I'm a little wobbly from

not eating and being sick. Just as I'm about to get into bed, Rose barrels through the door puffing out of breath.

"Where's the fire?" Daisy asks.

Rose smiles and chucks something on the bed. Daisy picks it up and her eyes go wide.

"A pregnancy test. Are you pregnant?" Daisy smiles.

Rose shakes her head.

"No way, but I reckon Serena is." Rose smiles.

All eyes come to me.

"What?! Uh-uh, nope. No way." I stutter.

"Did you and Wes have sex?" Rose asks, rolling her eyes at her own question.

"Of course we did." I answer.

"Did you have unprotected sex?" She asks.

"No. I get the shot every three months. It helps with my periods." I state.

"Okay, I will change my question. When was the last time you got a shot?" She asks.

I frown while trying to remember. The last time I remember was after my mother and brother's funeral. That can't be right, that was over nine months ago.

Rose smiles.

"Yeah, that's what I thought. Get in the bathroom and take the test." She orders. Daisy hands me the box.

I take it, my hands shaking nervously. I go to the bathroom and take care of business. I've barely flushed the toilet when the door is opened. Rose takes the test.

"You have to wait three minutes." I state.

Rose smiles.

"Not always." She says, turning the test around and showing me the little plus symbol.

"Congratulations! You're going to be a mamma." Rose smiles.

I feel myself become lightheaded and I wobble. I black out.

I awake in bed and sit up.

"What happened?" I ask.

"Well you found out that you're pregnant and then you passed out." Lily states.

"Shit. I'm pregnant." I whisper.

"Here, drink this." Daisy hands me a drink.

I sip it and scrunch my nose up in disgust.

"What's that?" I ask.

"It's a vitamin drink. It will help get some nutrients back into your body." she smiles.

"Well it tastes like crap." I state, putting it

back down.

"Honey." Rose calls. I look up to her.

"You doing okay? This is pretty big news, even in a normal situation. This situation is anything but normal." She says softly.

I sit for a moment and let the news sink in that I'm pregnant. I am pregnant with Wes' baby. I burst into tears and they all rush to hug me.

"I'm pregnant. How am I going to be a good mother? I can't even look after myself right now. The baby will never know their father, they will always have that part missing. I miss him so much. Why did he have to be taken away from me? He would have been a fantastic dad. Oh my god! I drank tequila! I got their father killed and now I've probably given the baby foetal alcohol syndrome." I wail hysterically.

"That's enough of that. Now don't be ridiculous. You have us and all of Satan's Outlaws to support and help you. Also, I used to drink a glass of wine every night throughout my pregnancies. It did my kids no harm." Penny states.

Lily, Rose, and Daisy turn to their mother and shake their heads.

"Yeah, cheers for that." Rose grunts.

"What?! It was different back then, you were allowed to do it." Penny defends. "What I am saying is that we are all here for you. You will make a fantastic mother because you are kind, caring, and strong. Now I know it's terribly sad that Wes will not be around to help or see his child grow, but you can tell this baby every day just how wonderful and magnificent their father was. Now here's the bit you need to do. You need to eat and you need to be stronger than you've ever been, because that little baby needs you." Penny pats my hand and leaves.

"Wow, your mom is good at pep talks." I state, sniffing and wiping my eyes.

"She had a lot of practice, Daisy was a hellion." Lily says teasingly.

Penny comes back a few minutes later with a huge tray of different foods.

"Here, let's see what you can stomach right now. Try the crackers, there are pretzels and plain crisps too. Whoops sorry, we are in America, I mean chips. There is some fizzy soda and some hard candies there as well. If all else fails you can hopefully stomach enough to get some sugar from them. I am going to pop to the pharmacy and get you some pregnancy vitamins too." She pats my cheek and turns to leave.

"Err Mum!" Rose calls out.

Penny sticks her head round the door.

"Yes?" She smiles.

"We are in lockdown and not allowed out

to, you know, to go shopping and shit. I don't think Serena is ready for the whole club to know yet." Rose states.

Penny pauses for a moment.

"You're right. I shall think of something. Don't worry, leave it with me." She smiles and leaves.

"Holy shit. I'm pregnant." I repeat to myself.

"That you are. I don't suppose you can guess how far along you are?" Lily asks.

"Um, no idea. We...well we were busy a lot." I smile.

"Well we will have to sneak you to a hospital to get you and the baby checked out." Daisy states.

"I don't want anyone knowing, not yet. I'm still trying to get my head around it." I sigh.

"Of course. Let's run you a bath. You can have a soak and a bit of peace to yourself." Rose says. She walks into the bathroom and starts running me a bath.

"We will leave you to it." They all stand to leave. Lily stops in the doorway.

"Um if you're okay with it, do you mind if I tell Blake? Wes was his brother and he is struggling. I think something like this will really help to lift his spirits." She asks hesitantly.

"Um, sure. If you think it will help him." I smile.

"Thanks. I'm sure it will. Now go and relax in the bath." She orders before shutting the door behind her.

I lay in the warm bath and sigh. I close my eyes and all I can see is a little boy with Wes' eyes and smile and my dark hair. I smile as the tears fall once again. I place my hand over my lower stomach. A piece of him, a piece of Wes, will forever be with me. I need to find the strength for his baby, our baby.

I cry in the bath and then I cry myself to sleep in bed. I lost the man I love but gained his baby to love. Life can be cruel, it can tear you apart. When all hope is lost, when you think there is no point in carrying on, life decides to throw you a small glimmer of hope. Life will throw you a small bit of glitter, shining in the depths of darkness. The hard part is catching that bit of glitter and making it shine and sparkle. The hard part is drowning out the darkness with nothing but its beautiful light.

CHAPTER TWENTY-SIX

Serena

I wake the next morning and my eyes are puffy from all of the crying. My head is throbbing but I feel okay. I feel different from every other morning I've woken up since it happened. The longing and the missing Wes is still there but now it's like I have a purpose again. I have a reason not to let myself get swallowed up by the darkness.

I get up and get dressed, deciding to head downstairs for something to eat. As soon as I open my door the smell of bacon hits me, making my stomach growl hungrily. I pat my stomach and head downstairs.

I walk into the loud kitchen and dining room and the kids are running riot and screaming chasing each other. I fiddle with my hands nervously as I make my way to the pot of coffee.

A hand touches my shoulder.

"Decaf." A deep voice whispers in my ear. I jump, nearly dropping the pot, and turn and look up at a smiling Blake. He rests his arm around me and gives me a squeeze.

"He would have made the best father." He sighs. "Just know that you won't be alone. Lily and I are here to help you in anyway we can."

I smile.

"Thanks Blake." I reach for the decaf pot. Blake winks at me and walks over to Lily and their baby girl Ivy.

"Oh honey!" Is screeched from Trudy, nearly making me spill my mug of coffee. She pulls me in for a hug. "So glad you are back down here. Let's get you fed." She leads me to all of the food and piles my plate sky high. I sit down, my eyes wide at how much is on my plate. I take a tentative bite of bacon, hoping that I don't throw up. It seems to be okay. I sigh with relief and practically shovel all of the bacon on the plate in my mouth. I moan. Being able to eat something that isn't making me throw up is the best feeling in the world.

"Mum, quick, fire up some more bacon. Serena's eating it all!" Rose teases.

"What?" I say with a mouthful. "It's the first thing that is actually staying down." I argue back.

"Oh I know, just teasing. Have you tried anything else?" Daisy asks as she sits next to me.

"No. I'm too scared that if I do I will be sick." I say honestly.

"Here, take these." Penny places two pills down on the table.

"Vitamins." She whispers.

I nod and take them. I finish eating, feeling like I'm going to explode. Rip walks in and his eyes focus on me. He nods his head to follow him. I look to Rose in question and she shoos me to follow him. Confused, I follow him down to his office.

Once inside he shuts the door. Rubble is standing there waiting.

"Err what's going on?" I ask, looking back and forth between them.

"Congratulations on the baby." Rip states, smiling.

I roll my eyes.

"So much for keeping it quiet."

"Don't complain. She had to tell me so that you can go to the hospital and get checked out. It's my club, it's my family, I always know what's going on." Rip shrugs.

"Okay, I understand that, but can we keep it quiet? Just until I can get used to the idea and I know that everything is okay?" I ask.

"Sure. Rubble knows because he is the one who's going to take you to the hospital to get checked out. You're leaving now, out of this side door." He informs me, holding open the door.

"Huh? Now?" I ask, dumbfounded.

"Yeah. Oh and wear this." He hands me a baseball cap.

I give him a look.

"It's the best disguise you've got right now." He answers.

"Fine." I sigh, putting the cap on.

I follow Rubble to the truck and pause, seeing Wes' truck parked up with the bullet holes in the door. I freeze and shiver.

"Serena." Rubble calls.

I look to him. His face is soft with concern.

"You okay?"

I swallow the lump in my throat and nod, blinking away my tears.

We get in the truck and I stare at my lap, not trusting myself to look out of the window as I will only look at the truck. Rubble's hand reaches out and holds mine. He gently strokes his thumb on mine soothingly.

He pulls off. Only when we are on the road does he let go.

"You're good to look out of the window now." He says quietly.

I look up and sigh.

"Thanks." I mutter.

He doesn't respond, he just looks straight ahead.

He is constantly checking his rear-view mirror to make sure we aren't being followed. I look behind me; there's nothing there. I breathe a sigh of relief.

"I wouldn't let anything happen to you." He informs me randomly.

"Uh, thanks. I'm just a little anxious." I smile.

"Understandable." He answers before going silent again.

We pull up into the hospital and he escorts me to the department where my appointment is. We sit in the waiting area. I don't miss the appreciative glances from the staff towards Rubble. I smile and shake my head.

"What?" He asks.

I look up at him and roll my eyes.

"Oh come on! You can't tell me you haven't noticed that practically everyone in here has been giving you the eye." I smile.

His face blank of emotion, he shrugs.

"I choose not to notice it. I'm not interested." He states nonchalantly.

"Okay Mr-playing-it-cool." I tease.

I catch his lips twitch and for a minute I think he might smile, but instead his face returns to its normal hard brooding expression.

"Miss...err...Smith. Miss Serena Smith?" A nurse calls.

I look to Rubble.

"No records." He states.

I get up and he follows me. I stop and turn. You...um...don't have to come in. I'm sure I will be safe." I state.

He just stares back at me and shakes his head. I huff and turn back around and enter the doctor's office.

"Welcome. How is mom-to-be feeling today?" The doctor smiles.

"I'm okay. I finally managed to keep some food down." I smile.

"Ahh, sickness is no fun is it? And Dad, how are you coping with it all?" She asks but doesn't let him answer. She leans in and loudly whispers. "Men are just like big children, they like to feel included in these things. We have to feed their egos a little." She giggles and winks. I look at Rubble who crosses his arms over his chest and just gives her a death glare.

"Ooo he's a broody one isn't he? Right Serena, can you pop those jeans off and put on the gown provided just behind that curtain. Then we can begin the internal ultrasound" She smiles.

"Internal?" I whisper.

"Yes, you're early in your pregnancy so it's the best way to get a good look at baby to determine how far along you are." She beams.

I nod and walk behind the curtain. Rubble goes to follow me but I hold my hand up.

"I don't think so. You stay this side of the curtain." I order.

"Come and wait with me honey! Don't be offended, a lot of women get body conscious when they are pregnant. Just you wait until the hormones kick right in midway through the pregnancy! She will be all over you like a rash. You'll be begging her to give you a break. Believe me." The doctor hoots with laughter while I die of embarrassment behind the curtain.

I come out and sit myself on the couch with Rubble stood next to me. I tug on his arm and pull him closer.

"Uh, up the head end please." I order.

He grunts and moves so he's standing by my head. The doctor covers me with a sheet and holds up large wand covered in jelly.

"Now this may feel a little uncomfortable." She smiles. "Just relax." She says before inserting the wand. I jolt slightly at the cold intrusion and instinctively grab hold of Rubble's hand.

She pushes and moves the wand around.

"I would like you to meet your healthy little baby. I'd say you look about ten weeks pregnant. Congratulations Mom and Dad." She smiles and turns the screen to face us.

I gasp as a tiny little blob wiggles and moves on the screen. I can just make out a nose and the tiniest arms and legs. I grip Rubble's hand so tight, trying to hold my emotions together.

The doctor pauses the frame.

"I just have to go and get some more printer paper for your scan pictures. I won't be a moment." She excuses herself.

I break when the door closes, no longer able to hold back the emotion. Rubble keeps hold of my hand and tries to calm me down by stroking the hair from my face. He leans in and kisses my head.

"It's okay, it will be okay." He whispers.

He hands me a tissue and I wipe my eyes. Sniffling, I apologise.

"I'm sorry you got stuck bringing me here and dealing with my outburst."

"You don't need to apologise for anything. I'm glad I came." He states. sincerely.

The doctor walks back in.

"Oh no deary, what's the matter?" She asks.

"Just hormones." Rubble answers for me. I smile up at him and mouth thank you. The doctor chats away while putting the paper in the machine. Rubble just gives me a chin lift in response.

The doctor prints off a couple of scan photos and hands them to Rubble.

"There you go Dad. Mom, off you pop to change." She states, helping me off of the couch.

I catch Rubble staring at the photos. There's no emotion on his face, he's just staring.

I change and place the baseball cap back on before I leave the room.

"Be safe. Here are some pamphlets with necessary information on. I wrote the date of your next appointment on that card along with my number, should you need me." She smiles and waves us off.

Rubble looks everywhere as he escorts us back to the truck.

On the drive back I'm less tense and I can't stop staring at the scan pictures.

"I'm still trying to work out what that is,

because I can't see no baby. It's just a blob." He says bluntly.

"What? The blob is the baby, it has tiny arms and legs right there. You see?" I say, holding up the picture.

He looks briefly and just shrugs.

"If you say so."

I smile and shake my head.

Once back at the house I notice that Rubble parks in front of the house this time, avoiding Wes' truck. As soon as we step inside the house they are like a swarm of bees surrounding us.

"Show us the scan."

"How far along are you?"

"Can they tell what it is yet?" They all ask.

"Alright, calm down. I'm ten weeks. Everything was fine. No, they can't tell me what it is yet." I answer whilst laughing.

Daisy looks to me and smiles.

"It's good to see you smiling." She whispers as she pulls me in for a hug.

"It feels good to be smiling." I whisper back.

Rubble walks off.

"Rubble wait!" I yell after him.

He stops and turns. I run to him.

"Thanks for today. Thanks for coming with me. I'm not sure I could have done it alone or with anyone else for that matter. Oh, and sorry for my mini breakdown too." I say honestly.

Rubble just nods.

"Anytime." He says before walking away.

CHAPTER TWENTY-SEVEN

Serena

Over the next few weeks it becomes easier for me to eat. I'm still sick in the morning and have some food trigger sickness but overall I manage to keep my food down.

My mood is improving slowly and there only seem to be some nights where I cry myself to sleep. I still have this longing and emptiness which I'm starting to realise will never completely go.

The whole of the Satan's Outlaws know about my pregnancy and I didn't tell them. It was just gossip that eventually reached everyone. I wasn't mad because it saved me doing it. I'm happy it's out there so I don't have to hide it.

I go and sit outside. Everyone is just getting a little fed up now about still being in lockdown. It may be a big house but it does get restrictive and there's only so much you can do.

Deciding to grab myself a snack I head to the kitchen. Just as I'm about to walk in I hear arguing.

"She deserves to know!" What sounds like Rose shouts.

"Woman, she's been through enough, I'm not showing her this letter right now." I hear Rip defend.

"She is a grown woman and needs to know about it. If you don't tell her, I will." Rose threatens.

"You're a pain in my ass." Rip mutters.

I walk in and fold my arms across my chest.

"So what should I know?" I ask.

They both turn to me and Rose smiles an 'I'm getting my way' smile to Rip. He rolls his eyes and reaches into his back pocket. He pulls out a letter and hands it too me.

"It's a letter. It was left on the windscreen of one of our trucks when we went to the grocery store. It's addressed to you. It's from Jesús." He states angrily.

My hand shakes as I take the letter.

"I should read this." I say, walking out of the kitchen and heading back outside.

Sitting down I open the letter to read. My

stomach coils with anxiety.

Mi hermana,

I hope you have forgiven me for what I had to do. Believe me, it was not easy. You should know that I didn't plan on killing your lover, just whoever you brought as protection. It was a mere unfortunate incident.

As I am being honest with you, I suppose I should let you know that my men where the ones involved with your mamma and hermano's accident. I am sorry but I couldn't have the woman who stole my padre's affection live well and be happy while my madre suffered a life of misery and pain.

You see, life is all about balance, good vs evil. I was merely keeping that balance. It was a duty, a code of conduct if you will. Now see, I will not harm you in any way, my dear hermana. We are the innocent ones caught up in the crossfire of chaos. We are the same soul that has been torn apart. We have a connection like no other.

I shall warn you. You must know that I'm coming for the Satan's soon. Soon there will be a devastating war. This letter is to make sure that you keep safe, keep hidden. Once I have killed everyone that is in my path, I shall rescue you.

Just think of the power and the fear. Hermano and hermana ruling the world!

Be ready hermana. The war is coming and I'm

taking what is mine, what is ours, to rule.

Your one and only hermano,

Jesús

My stomach recoils. I lean over and empty the contents of my stomach. He will kill everyone. He will stop at nothing until he gets what he wants. I get up and go in search of Rip. I find him and nod in the direction of his office.

Once inside he closes the door behind us.

"Did you read it?" I ask.

He nods.

"Yeah I did." He states and crosses his arms over his chest.

"Well? What are you going to do about it?" I ask, slamming the letter down on the desk.

"It's all arranged. It's fine. We have everything sorted. You don't need to worry." He says calmly.

I'm anything but calm right now because I have seen firsthand what my brother is capable of.

"Don't worry?! I have seen exactly what my brother is capable of. I watched as he shot down two of his own men for stupid reasons. Then I watched as his men shot at Wes multiple times. I watched as his orders got Wes killed. I watched him die right before me. Now don't you fucking tell me not to worry. Dio mi dà forza!" I seethe.

Rip walks towards me and wraps his arms around me.

"I promise you it will all be okay. We have a plan and you and everyone else will be safe. Trust us." He states. "I will let you know what the plan is soon, I promise."

I step back and sigh.

"I don't believe in promises anymore. Nothing is certain. I will only stop worrying when all of this shit is over." I bite back and storm out of his office.

He may think that he can outplay Jesús, that he can beat him, but I'm not so convinced. Rip has emotions, Rip has a conscience, Jesús doesn't. That makes him all the more dangerous. I wouldn't be surprised if Jesús lost every man he had. He wouldn't even blink, he would just brush it off as a minor inconvenience. That is where Rip needs to watch his back. He needs to watch everything and every move Jesús takes.

You never see the darkness. The darkness makes sure you can't see it. It surrounds you, makes you blind to any danger, even if it's right in front of you. Jesús is the all-consuming darkness.

****

There are whispers and the brothers are attending more and more church meetings. We all notice and the tension rises within the house. I'm not sure if it would be easier for Rip to just say which day is the day. Then at least we'd have something to prepare for; the not knowing is more stressful.

I'm curled up in the window seat reading when I see a very flashy looking car pull up out front. A devastatingly handsome and sharply dressed man gets out and adjusts his cuffs. He screams power and money. He's tall, broad, and his muscular physic is visible even through his suit. He has closely cut black hair, beautiful dark skin, a strong jaw, and a light dusting of stubble surrounding his delectable lips.

"Who is that?" I ask Patty.

"Oh honey, that's Dreads. He is a fine piece of man. He's so hot and also technically my boss, although I never really see him." She answers.

"Ooo is that Dreads?" Lily asks, leaning over us to look out of the window.

"Yup." Patty swoons.

"Move! Let me see him!" Rose yells and dives over us.

"Oh he is very handsome." Even Daisy swoons.

He removes his shades and looks up to see us all with our faces pressed against the window.

"Oh crap, he's seen us." Rose mutters, yet none of us move.

He gifts us with a smile and a wink. I swear they all lose it. They're squealing like teenagers.

"You guys are insane." I smile.

"Oh come on, he is beautiful. Did you see that smile?! Wow!" Rose fans herself.

We all laugh. Rip comes up behind her without her knowing.

"The husband is behind me, isn't he?" Rose winces.

We all nod, snickering.

She spins around slowly to face a pissed off looking Rip. Whoops.

"Hey biker boy." Rose sings.

Rip leans in close.

"You enjoying the view sweetheart? Enjoying looking at another man, a man that ain't your husband?" He asks.

"Maybe just a little." She says, pinching her index finger and thumb close together.

He grunts.

"Seems like I will need to remind you that you only have eyes for me. I reckon you'll need reminding that it's my mouth and my cock that make you scream my name." He threatens, leaning even closer to her mouth.

"You're mine sweetheart." He states before crashing his mouth onto hers. Their kiss is hot passionate and I feel like I'm intruding on a very personal moment. Rip suddenly breaks the kiss.

"Mine." He growls before walking off, leaving a very aroused and flushed Rose behind.

"Wow, who knew we would get a live porno?" Lily snorts.

"Bastard! He played me good. Damn. I shall get him back later." Rose winks.

"You guys need to control your libido." I laugh.

"Oh come on! You can't say that beautiful dark and delicious man did not make you want to throw yourself at him? Man, we were all practically dribbling." Rose points out.

I laugh and shake my head.

"Don't get me wrong, he is very handsome, extremely so, but not for me. I hate to lower the mood but I'm not really there yet. You know?" I shrug.

"Ahh shit. Now I feel like a dick." Rose mutters. "So sorry honey." She apologises.

I smile.

"It's all good, You all made me laugh for a while. It was great watching you all fan girl over him." I chuckle.

"You ain't kidding! I mean, a man like that, I reckon he has an impressive wang." Lily states.

I laugh.

"An impressive wang?"

"Well yeah. A man that oozes that hotness and power isn't going to have a maggot penis! It's going to be an all powerful member." She giggles.

We all laugh.

"I reckon he knows exactly what he's doing in the bedroom department too." Daisy adds.

"Oh yeah. I bet he's all dominant and shit." Patty nods.

"I bet he would finger bang like a damn marksman." Rose sighs. "Pure precision, taking care to always hit his target."

We cry with laughter.

"Oh my god you guys, you kill me. You already have the hottest guys. I bet you have nothing to complain about in the bedroom department." I point out.

They all exchange a knowing look. They are clearly all very satisfied in the bedroom department.

"Exactly my point." I laugh. "I'm going to

get a drink from the kitchen, do you want anything?" I ask.

"Nah we're good." Rose answers.

I walk into the kitchen and open the fridge to grab a bottle of water. I can hear heated words being exchanged in the room where they hold 'church'. I tiptoe and stand outside, listening in.

"Saturday." A deep velvet voice says.

"Agreed." Rip answers.

Suddenly the door handle starts to turn and I try to move quickly away while doing my best to act like I'm not eavesdropping. I'm staring intently at the label of my bottle like it holds the secret to cure the world's problems.

"Serena?" I hear Rip say. My head snaps up and I smile.

"Hey. I'm just, um, getting a drink of water." I say, a little high pitched.

Rip's mouth twitches, fighting a smile. He blatantly knows I was listening in.

"Miss." The deep voice calls.

I turn to look behind me and my eyes meet beautiful green eyes.

"Hi." I breathe. Apparently I have forgotten how to talk properly.

"Christ." Rip mutters.

Dreads smiles a sad smile.

"Miss, I'm sorry to hear about the loss of Wes. You have my deepest condolences. Between myself and the Satan's Outlaws, I can promise that those responsible will pay." He states with certainty and sincerity. I know he means every word.

"Thank you." I nod.

He takes my hand in his and places a kiss.

"Pleasure to meet you Serena." He states before walking away. Rip follows, shaking his head.

I stand still, almost not wanting to wash my hand ever again. He has this almost celebrity presence about him. I feel like I've just met my high school boy band crush.

"Seriously? What does that guy have that makes chicks go like this?!" Khan complains.

"The man just has it, and a lot more of it than most men. We don't stand a chance when you have a guy like that around." Mammoth laughs.

I walk back into the lounge and see the girls with their faces pressed up against the window again, watching Dreads leave. I decide not to mention that he spoke to me, I don't think they'd appreciate it much.

CHAPTER TWENTY-EIGHT

Serena

It's Saturday and I can't help but feel tense. They said Saturday in the meeting. Something is happening and it's happening today.

I wanted to ask but I haven't seen Rip. All of the guys have been absent. I asked Rose but she just said club business, even she doesn't know.

I've had a restless night's sleep. I look at the clock to see it's 4am. I groan and decide to get up and go to the bathroom. As I come out of my room I can hear voices coming from downstairs. I pause and lean over the banister to try and see who it is.

It's Rip and the guys; they're loading up and getting ready to leave. I quickly creep back into my room and get changed. I look out of my window and see them loading up the trucks. Quickly I move down the stairs, being careful not to be seen. I reach the bottom and see a backpack left behind. I open it and inside is a gun, ammo, a large knife, and a walkie talkie. I grab it. I'm just about to sneak out when I hear footsteps approaching.

"Alright I'm coming. I'm sure there were more than five bags, let me check." I quickly move and hide, pressing myself up against the wall. I watch as Rubble comes in and looks around. I don't move or make a sound. He is about to look where I am hiding but is called from outside.

"Fuck it." He mutters before leaving.

I let out a breath and go to follow them.

"Are you sure you want to go with them?" A voice asks.

I jump and spin around to see Max. He wheels himself forward.

"It isn't going to be safe and it's definitely not something you're gonna want to witness darlin'." He states.

I hear the engines start up and I look to the door and back to Max.

"I have to. I have to be the one to end him." I reply before running outside.

I keep low. I notice all of the trucks are taken, all but one: Wes' truck. I swallow a lump and take a deep breath, jumping in the truck.

I'm relived that it's been cleaned. Tears fall but I quickly wipe them away, checking the sun visor for keys but with no such luck.

"Come on." I mutter. I lean over and open the glove box. Nothing. I slam it shut. "Damn it." I slam my hands on the steering wheel.

There's a tap on the truck. I look out to see Max holding the keys. I open the door and jump out.

"I swear if anything happens to you I will never forgive myself, but you're the only one who can get close enough to him to end it. He deserves to die, for Wes. He needs to die." Max states, chucking me the keys. "Go now before I change my fuckin' mind."

I lean over and kiss him on the cheek and jump in the truck. The guys have just left but I can catch them up. I start the truck and screech out of the driveway, remembering to keep my lights off. I see the lights up ahead.

"Come on Serena." I mutter to calm myself.

I know they will question why I would risk mine and my baby's lives, but the answer is simple. He took Wes from me. He took my baby's father from them. I will never be okay. I will not rest until I know that he has paid for destroying my life. Brother or not, I have to try for my sanity.

I keep back a little so I'm not noticed. I

realise that they aren't going to Jesús house. I frown but keep following. Eventually they pull over up ahead. I quickly tuck in. I lean forward over the steering wheel and squint, trying to see what they are doing.

There's a knock at the window which makes me scream. Rip stands there with his arms crossed over his chest, looking pissed. I sigh and open the door.

"Hi. Fancy seeing you here." I try acting innocent.

Rip rolls his eyes.

"Go the fuck home." He orders.

"No." I snap.

His eyes flash with anger. I swallow nervously.

"Serena, this is fuckin' war, not a play date. It is not safe. Go the fuck home." He grits.

"I'm not going anywhere. I'm the only one who can get close to Jesús. He took Wes from me! I need to kill him, he needs to pay." I argue back.

Rip grits his jaw.

"You stay in the fuckin' truck. You don't get out until we come and get you. Am I clear?!" He snaps.

I nod.

"Follow us but stay the fuck back." He says

before slamming the truck door shut.

Rip walks off behind me and jumps in a truck.

"How in the hell did he get behind me?" I say to myself as he overtakes and drives ahead.

I follow them as they stop by Jesús' house entrance. I stop and tuck the truck further back from them like Rip ordered.

I watch as they pile out. There are some trucks further up that aren't the Satans'.

"Dreads." I mutter to myself, watching as they follow the Satan's Outlaws.

They move with military precision. They pause and wait for something. There's a loud explosion which makes me jump. I gasp. Under the cover and surprise of the smoke they file in.

The sound of gunfire fills the air.

"Oh shit." I mutter.

I sit nervously tapping the steering wheel and biting my lip, nearly drawing blood. I hear shouting and more gunfire. I wonder how they are getting away with this. There has been no sign of police. Surely the houses in the distance can hear this?

The guns shots sound closer. I grab the bag nervously and pull out the gun and ammo. I try to load it but my hands are shaking. I drop some bullets on the floor.

"Fuck." I mutter. I reach down to pick up the bullets.

As I come back up I see Jesús is standing by the passenger side window. He's smiling. I scream. He opens the door and jumps in.

"Mi hermana, I knew you'd come for me. Drive! Rápido!" He states.

I still sit frozen with the gun in my hand, wondering if this is my moment. Is this my opportunity to kill him and end it all?

Jesús looks to me and sees I'm not moving. He looks down to the gun and tuts, his head shaking.

"Mi hermana." He says, grabbing the gun.

He takes the safety off.

"Silly mi hermana. You must always know how to use a gun correctly if you intend to use it." He sneers. "Drive." He orders again. This time his voice is low and threatening. He knows why I've come here, he knows what I intend to do. But now he knows, instead of me ending his life, will it be him ending mine?

CHAPTER TWENTY-NINE

Rip

We pull up, ready to enter Jesús property. Everyone is armed, bracing for what is about to come. The only thing at the back of my mind is Wes. This was already a war but now it's a personal fuckin' vendetta, even more so with Serena sat in the truck awaiting payback. This is payback for her and for their unborn baby that Wes will never meet. This is the day that Jesús will be begging for redemption.

Rubble sets up the explosives on the gates. He gives us the signal to step back. He presses a little button on a small remote and boom, the gates blow clean off, taking out some of the wall with them. Under the cover of the dust we charge forward and scan the perimeter.

With Dreads' men following behind us, a few of Jesús guards come running towards us. I grab one before he has a chance to shoot and run my blade across his neck. I chuck him to the floor. Gunshots ring out as our men run inside the house. I walk with purpose, not panicking or running. I know where my target will be and I'm heading straight for him.

"Rip! Three o'clock!" Khan yells.

I quickly turn and throw my knife at the guy who is ready to fire. The blade hits him right between the eyes and he drops to the floor. I bend down and, placing my boot on his head, I pull out my blade and wipe the blood remnants on the guy's shirt.

"Aww man, that sound gets me every time." Khan gags.

"Shut up you pussy." I sigh.

"Cover me, I'm going after Jesús. I'm gonna bring that motherfucker out here and he's gonna pay." I grit.

Khan nods. Dreads walks up to me with his gun aimed. "I'm coming with you. We will drag that piece of shit out here together."

"Fine by me." I agree.

We both walk through the extravagant house, checking each room as we go.

"The cleaner said he is always in the den in the basement." I state.

We find the door and slowly and carefully make our way down the stairs. We can hear a TV.

Checking no one else is down here we enter the den.

Jesús is sat there in an armchair smoking a cigarette and laughing at the movie he is watching.

"Welcome to mi casa, gentlemen. Please feel free to help yourselves to a drink at my bar." He points and starts laughing at the movie again.

"Jesús, get the fuck up and come and face your fuckin' fate!" I growl, aiming my gun at him.

He stands and open his arms wide.

"You have me. I am not afraid to meet my fate, but are you, Rip?" Jesús questions.

"Go fuck yourself. I make my own fate. When that day comes I shall fuckin' embrace it." I snap back.

Jesús smiles.

"I see. People like us, Rip, and even you Dreads, we think we have control over our fate. We have no control. What is it they say? You reap what you sow?"

"When that day comes we will face it, but that day isn't today. Today it's your turn to face your consequences." Dreads states calmly.

"Well then, I'm sure you won't mind if I pour myself a little drink before you make me face my consequences." He rolls his eyes.

He walks to the bar and starts making himself a fuckin' cocktail.

"I bet you thought that because I'm Mexican I would be pouring myself a tequila. Am I right?" He smiles, taking a drag of his cigarette. "Well, you're wrong. I am a whiskey sour man. Classy and sophisticated, yet manly." He states, laughing to himself while making it.

Once he's finished making it he holds up his glass.

"There, perfección." He says before taking a sip and moaning. "Delicioso."

"Let's go. You've had your final drink now let's go." I growl, losing my patience.

"Oh, one more thing." He pauses and lights another cigarette. "You don't decide my fate, I do."

A guy jumps up from behind the bar with a machine gun firing at us. We dive out of the way as quickly as we can. We stay low and hidden until the gunfire ceases.

When it does I peer around the corner to see the guy attach another round of ammo on. Taking my chance I aim and fire. The bullet hits him straight in the side of his head. Panting, I go to stand. My leg gives out from under me. I look down and notice I've been shot in my thigh.

"Shit." I hiss.

"Dreads, you good?" I yell.

"Yeah but I've been hit in the damn shoulder. You?" He yells back.

"Fuckin' thigh." That mother fucker got away. We had him and he got away.

Dreads walks over to me and holds out his hand to help me up. He helps me up the stairs to find the others. The house is carnage, there are things smashed, bullet holes, and dead bodies litter the floor and the stairs.

We get outside and everyone is waiting for us.

"Where is Jesús?" Khan asks.

"Oh he's just coming now, he's grabbing us the fuckin' first aid kit." I yell sarcastically.

"He fuckin' got away didn't he." I mutter, sitting on the step.

"We haven't seen him so he can't have got far." Mammoth states.

It hits me.

"Serena." I state.

Rubble, Mammoth, and the others run out of the grounds. Dreads gives me a look. Before they even make it back we both know what they are going to say.

"She's gone!" Rubble pants as he runs back.

"Fuck!" I yell. "The mother fucker played us. He fuckin' knew! The son of a bitch." I seethe.

"Take me and Dreads to Rose now. You all go and search for Wes' truck while we get patched up. Then we will join you in the hunt." I order.

I should have just sent her home. Fuck! I will not have her death on my conscience as well as Wes'.

CHAPTER THIRTY

Serena

I feel a mixture of anger and fear that Jesús is next to me. We're in the truck he had Wes killed in.

"Where am I driving you to?" I ask.

"Us, mi hermana. You are driving us to the boarder. I have men and transport waiting for us there. Then we can live happily in my home in Mexico, it's very beautiful." He smiles.

"I'm not going with you Jesús. I have a life here, I am staying here." I answer honestly, hoping that my honesty doesn't get me killed.

"You've lost weight. You look ill mi hermana." He points out, completely disregarding my answer.

"I have. I haven't been eating properly. I've been mourning Wes." I grit through my teeth.

"Oh so you're still mad at me for that? I thought you might have calmed down a bit by now." He shrugs.

I slam the breaks on and pull over to the side of the road. I turn in my seat to face him.

"Calm down? Calm down! Are you even hearing yourself right now?!" I fume. I grip my hair and take a deep breath. "You killed the man I love, the man I would have married, the man I wanted to grow old with! The father of my baby!" I yell as tears fall freely down my face. I am no longer scared, only angry.

"I didn't technically kill him." He shrugs.

My mouth drops open in shock at his response.

"You're pregnant?" He asks, staring at my stomach.

"Yeah." I answer, wiping my tears.

"You love this baby." He states, staring at my stomach. "You know, I never felt love." He adds.

"Don't give me your sob story now, okay? It's all a little too late." I say and shake my head.

"It's not a sob story, but it may make you realise why I am a monster." He shrugs.

"My padre, our padre, was only ever in love with your mother. You know this, you know my Madre was depressed, on drugs, and drank constantly. Well that was my life. The niñera, the nanny, even she didn't cuddle me or give me love. She was there out of fear, all of the staff were. Mis amigos weren't really mis amigos. They were there because of the power and fear Padre commanded. I am a product of fear, of being surrounded by fear. Money and fear will give you everything you could want. They could until I found you." He says honestly.

I shake my head.

"Don't. Don't make me feel sorry for you. You killed my mamma, my brother, and my lover. Why?!" I scream. "Why would you do that?!"

He looks out of the window and a small smile plays on his face.

"Because I wanted something that was just mine, I wanted someone to like me and love me. You have to love me because we are related, and with them out of the picture all of that love would be for me, I wouldn't have to share you." He states.

"Do you have any idea how insane that sounds? I hate you for what you've done. You have destroyed my life. Why would I want a brother like you?" I spit.

"Get out of the car." He orders quietly.

"No." I refuse.

"I said get out of the fucking car!" He yells angrily. I jump and quickly search for the handle to get out.

I stand on the side of the road and he gets out. He walks towards me and stops a few feet away. He just looks at me.

He holds out the gun to me. I look at the gun and then look at him.

"Take it." He demands.

I reach out slowly, wondering if this is some kind of trick. I take the gun.

"It's fully loaded. I said I would decide my own fate, mi hermana." He says solemnly.

I look at the gun and aim it at him, my hands shaking.

He smiles,

"It's okay, mi hermana. Just know that I am sorry for the pain I caused you. I just wanted a sister." He apologises.

Tears fall down my face and the gun in my hand shakes even more. I want him dead. I need him dead, for Wes.

He looks at me with all of the sadness and deadness that's behind his eyes. I place my finger on the trigger. I move the gun at the last second and fire. I scream angrily at myself and fall to my knees, sobbing.

"You didn't kill me." He says in disbelief.

I sob, my shoulders shaking. I've let Wes,

my mamma, and my brother down. I could have got vengeance today, but I couldn't even bring myself to kill him. I couldn't bring myself to kill a man who has killed so many and probably will continue to do so.

He crouches down and pulls my hands from my face. He looks into my pained eyes.

"Mi hermana, I shall never forget this moment. I will hold it in my dead cold heart for everyday it is beating. You are the good to my evil. You are life's balance." He states before kissing the top of my head.

"Just go. Go now to Mexico and never come back. Never step anywhere near me, the Satan's Outlaws, or even this state." I croak.

He nods and picks up the gun. He lifts it and aims it at me. I gasp.

"Are you seriously going to kill me after I just spared your life?! You really are insane." I say. I'm stunned.

He wipes the corners of his mouth and smiles. He shrugs and then shoots. Pain sears through my shoulder. I scream and fall back, clutching my wound. He walks to me and crouches down next to me.

"I am sorry, mi hermana, but I cannot have my enemies thinking I am weak. I don't want them knowing my weakness is you. If word got out that I spared your life, it would be dangerous for me and I suppose for you." He states, pulling out a cigarette and lighting it.

He takes a couple of drags, looking around the quiet deserted road. I pant through my pain and try and sit up. He looks up ahead and smiles.

"Ahh, your cavalry have arrived. I shall miss Texas." He sighs. "It has been fun, now I must leave you. I'm sorry for what I am about to do." He apologises.

He rears back and hits me over the head with the butt of the gun. My vision blurs and I can no longer keep myself upright. I feel myself starting to black out.

"Te amo, mi hermana." I hear whispered before the darkness takes over.

****

I awake in a hospital room. The bright lights hurt my eyes and there's that familiar smell of disinfectant. My head is pounding. I try to move but wince when I feel a sharp pain in my shoulder.

I let my eyes adjust to the light. Squinting, I look around the room; it's empty. Carefully I sit myself up. Feeling woozy and thirsty I see a jug of water and a cup next to the bed. I try to use my good arm to pour myself a drink but my arm shakes with weight of the jug and I drop it. The water goes everywhere.

The door swings open and Mammoth stands there. He gives me a smile and walks in and picks up the jug.

"You know if you wanted some water you could have just asked. There's no point throwing it all over the floor." He smiles.

I give him a tight smile back.

"Just feeling thirsty." I reply.

"Yeah, I got that. Let me go and tell Pres and the others that you're awake. I only stuck my head in because I heard the noise as I was walking back from the canteen." He winks, handing me a bottle of water.

Taking it I smile.

"Thanks." I take a long sip which soothes my dry throat. "Hang on, you said get Pres and the rest. Who is here?" I ask.

"Everyone. The women, Penny, Ben, the brothers." He shrugs.

"But why?" I ask.

He laughs and shakes his head.

"Because you're family." He says like I'm stupid.

"But it's over. I don't need to be protected anymore and, well, Wes isn't with us either. You owe me nothing, your duty of watching me is over." I state.

Mammoth perches his large frame on the side of the bed.

"Here is what you need to get when it comes to the Satan's Outlaws, you were welcomed in as part of the family the moment that Wes declared you were his. Even with him gone, that doesn't stop you being a part of the Satan's, part of the family. We will always look out for you and your baby. It's what families do, it's what Wes would want us to do." He says, patting my leg.

He stands and turns to leave, stopping when he reaches the door.

"So if you were trying to get rid of us it's unlucky for you. Your ass is stuck with us." He laughs as he leaves.

I smile a warm feeling in my heart, knowing I'm not completely alone. I know that me and my baby will not be alone.

CHAPTER THIRTY-ONE

Serena

The nurse came by to check mine and the baby's stats. All was healthy and fine. I was expecting questions as to why a pregnant woman was in hospital with concussion and a bullet in her shoulder, but apparently when you're part of the Satan's Outlaws you don't get any questions.

The door opens and in walks Rip. He stands at the foot of the bed with his arms crossed over his chest like he owns the damn hospital.

"How are you feeling?" He asks.

"Like I've been hit over the head and shot." I answer with a small smile.

"You want to tell me what happened?" He asks.

I look away. Do I risk it and tell him that I couldn't do it? Do I tell him that I couldn't kill Jesús because I'm weak? Or do I lie and say I tried?

"Serena." He calls.

My eyes flick to his and his ice blue eyes stare back, awaiting my answer. I swallow nervously.

"He got in the truck and told me to drive. He took the gun and held it in his lap. We, um, talked. I got angry and pulled over."

"You got angry with him?" Rip interrupts, a smile playing on his lips.

I nod.

"Yeah, he was apologising for Wes, Mamma, and my brother. I laid into him. He didn't really argue back. He just told me to get out of the truck." I pause.

"And then what? You need to tell me, Serena." Rip pushes.

"He, um, well he gave me the gun." Rip looks taken aback. "He knew I was there to kill him. He said he was in control of his fate, or something like that anyway." I brush off. "I held the gun up and aimed it at him but my hands were shaking terribly. I tried, I really tried to do it. Honestly I did. I wanted him dead, I still do. But I just couldn't bring myself to do it. I crumbled to the floor and he took hold of the gun." I whisper, too afraid to look him in the eye. I feel like I have betrayed the Satan's Outlaws, betrayed Wes.

"Serena look at me." Rip demands.

I look up at him.

"I get why you couldn't kill him. Not only was he biologically your brother, but also he was standing there at close range, facing you. No normal person could kill someone like that. Not everyone is capable of murdering someone and you are one of those people. Now tell me why Jesús didn't kill you? Because I know damn well he would have no hesitation killing anyone else." He questions.

"He shot me in the shoulder and knocked me out so people wouldn't use me as his weakness or use me to get to him. He left for Mexico and is never returning. He is gone." I inform him.

"I will keep that bit of information to myself. He is right, if people found out he had a weakness they would use you to get to him." He agrees. "Who knew Jesús had a heart." He mutters.

He leaves me alone with my thoughts. Now the fear of Jesús is gone, the fear of being attacked, I guess I should go back to how life was before I met Wes. My florist shop and me in my house alone.

*****

The hospital let me go home two days later because they are satisfied that I'm recovering well. I catch a cab back to my house. I didn't call on any of the Satan's Outlaws because they were all getting back to their own lives and moving back into their houses. I wasn't about to become a burden. I pay the cab driver and walk up to my house. Unlocking the door I shove it open with the post piled behind it.

Walking through the house I see Wes' jacket hanging on the coat hook. I lean into it and smell it. The smell of him brings a calmness and a wave of emotion. I go to pour myself a drink. I open the fridge and there is Wes' beer. I take a bottle of water and quickly close the fridge. Deciding I should go for a lie down I head upstairs. There in the bathroom are some of Wes' toiletries. I avoid looking at them and wash my face, deciding to shut the curtains and climb into bed.

I grab Wes' t-shirt which he had chucked on top of the wash basket and carefully put that on. The smell of him envelopes me. I climb into bed and finally I let the tears fall that I had been holding back.

I must have cried myself to sleep because the next thing I know I'm being woken by banging and crashing downstairs. As quickly as I can I creep out of bed and grab my brother's baseball bat that I keep under the bed. I tip toe down the stairs.

I realise that the sound is coming from the kitchen. I move as quickly as I can holding the bat. I wish I could hold it higher but my shoulder hurts too much so crotch shots it is.

"Get out of my fucking house now or I will beat your ass." I yell, making the person jump and stand up from behind the counter.

"Rubble?!" I say, stunned.

"Hey. Rip, well, the women ordered me to bring over some groceries for you. They should be here themselves soon. Sorry if I scared you. I did call your name when I came in but you were fast asleep so I left you be. I was just trying to put these potatoes away but the bag split and I knocked over your saucepan. Sorry." He apologises.

"No, it's…um…fine. I…how did you get in?" I ask.

He reaches into his pocket and pulls out a spare key; the key I had given Wes. He places it on the side.

"I should get going before they all descend on the place." He jokes but doesn't smile.

"Okay. Thanks for bringing me the groceries, it's appreciated and a nice surprise."

"No worries." He says, giving me a chin lift

before leaving and closing the door behind him.

Now my heart has calmed down I decide to make myself a coffee. I open the cupboard and see that they even got me some fresh coffee. I look at the label. Decaf. I groan. Coffee is the first thing I'm going to miss while being pregnant.

I fill up the coffee machine and click it on. There's a banging at the door. I smile because I know it's the girls.

As I open the door Lily, Rose, Patty, and Daisy pile through. Lily hands over baby Ivy to me as she passes.

"I am breaking my neck for a pee!" She yells.

"Lily! You can't just dump Ivy on Serena, she is recovering from being shot!" Daisy yells after her.

"I'm okay. Don't worry." I assure her.

I look down at the cute little bundle in my arms. She is staring up at me with a 'who the hell are you' expression on her little face.

"Hey beautiful girl." I coo.

She smiles, giving me a big gummy smile.

"Oh my! Aren't you the cutest little princess." I smile back as she smiles more.

"Oh yeah, she loves the compliments. She is just like her mother. Aren't you? Yes you are!" Rose says in a funny voice.

Lily comes out and sighs.

"Have to say, your bladder is never the same after having a baby."

She takes Ivy and kisses her cheeks.

"So um, why are you guys here?" I ask, walking back into the kitchen to pour myself a coffee. "Oh and thanks for the groceries. Let me know how much I owe you for them." I say before taking a sip of coffee. "Oh sorry, did you guys want one?" I offer.

"Sure but I will make it, you sit down and rest." Patty orders.

"We are here because you are family and family help each other out. You left the hospital without telling any of us. Rubble was supposed to come in and put the groceries in without you knowing but of course you were already home so that plan had to change." Rose tuts. "Why didn't you call one of us to help you home?"

"I didn't want to burden you all. Wes is gone and I have to get used to life on my own. You all have your own lives to live, the last thing you need to deal with is a moaning mourning pain in your ass." I snort.

"Um, yes we do. Moan to us, let us help you. Hell! We love that shit and we're good at it too. Between all of us we've been through more shit that the whole entire series of soap opera." Patty affirms.

I look at all of them and they all smile and nod. I hold my hands up and sigh.

"Fine." I relent. "But I will warn you now, I'm better but I'm still having a meltdown over a lot of things."

"We know. We can see you've been crying again. You will. You will cry a lot more because you miss him. You will also cry a lot more due to your hormones. But we will be here to help you. You are not completely alone." Rose assures.

Of course at that moment I start crying. They all jump to their feet and carefully hug me, comforting me.

"Oh god I'm sorry. This is all so overwhelming. I didn't really have friends growing up and now I have all of you and it's amazing and lovely and just, well, just so surreal. I never imagined even knowing this many people let alone having you as a friend, so thank you." I sniffle.

"Wow, honey. That's enough to nearly set us all crying with our own waterworks." Patty says, blinking her tears away.

"Sorry." I laugh.

We all sit in the living room and let baby Ivy lay on the soft carpet. Lily is desperately trying to get her to crawl.

"God damn it Lily! She will do it when she's

ready." Rose complains.

"It said in the baby books to encourage them so I'm encouraging her." Lily snaps back.

"Um, there is something I need to tell you, tell all of you." Daisy says nervously. They look to one another.

Daisy looks at me and I smile and nod, remembering what Wes had said.

"Well, um, Carter and I eloped and got married a while ago. We had this big wedding reception planned but under the circumstance we have decided not to have it." She smiles sadly.

"What?! You buggered off to Vegas and got married?" Lily screeches.

"Um, yeah." Daisy winces, waiting for her reaction.

"Why didn't you tell us? That's amazing news! Mum will kill you but oh that is amazing!" Lily pulls Daisy in for a hug. Rose and Patty do the same.

"Why have you cancelled the reception? Wes wouldn't want you to do that, he would have wanted you to have it. You deserve it. Your family deserve it." I point out.

"I just didn't want to upset anyone or make it feel like we don't care. The reception was meant to be in two weeks' time and that is still so soon after Wes." She sighs.

I get up and walk to her. I hold her hands in mine.

"Do it, please. He would have wanted you too. Plus I think everyone needs a celebration right now." I insist.

She smiles and nods.

"Okay. Well, I guess I better call Carter."

They all scream excitedly, making poor Ivy jump. I laugh and pick Ivy up and bounce her in my arms.

I look down at Ivy and smile, trying to hold it all together. This isn't the right moment to have a breakdown. I can cry to myself later. A mixture of happiness and sadness fill me. I have longed to have a family and friends like this, but it's so bitter sweet because Wes isn't here sharing it with me.

CHAPTER THIRTY-TWO

Serena

I'm standing in my florist staring into space. I don't even hear the chime above the door ring as a customer enters.

"Hey! Serena." A deep voice bellows.

I jump and look to see Mammoth smiling.

"Where were you? Anywhere nice?" He laughs.

I shake my head, smiling.

"Sorry, I was completely away with it. No. I was nowhere." I sigh. "What can I do for you?" I ask.

"I want to send some flowers, sort of 'I'm sorry' type flowers?" He asks.

I smile.

"Sure. Do you know if they have a favourite colour or specific flower? That will give you brownie points." I wink.

"Um shit, no. She likes bright colours. She hates dull things and always wears bright colours." He mutters almost nervously.

It's cute seeing this mountain of a man splutter with embarrassment over a lady.

I gather up some bright red and pink roses. They're romantic yet a great flower for an apology bouquet. I add a few leafy stems.

I wrap it all together for him.

"Would you like to write a card?" I ask.

He nods and takes the card. I peer over to see what he has written. 'Give me a chance'. He puts it in the envelope and seals it. I place it nicely in the bouquet and hand it to him.

"There, all done." I smile.

"Great, how much?" He asks.

"Oh, um, mates rates. Let's say twenty dollars." I smile.

He hands over fifty dollars.

"Mates tips." He winks as he leaves.

I wonder who the flowers were for? I guess he's keeping it close to his chest for now. I hope she forgives him for whatever it is he has done.

The day goes by pretty slowly. Even though I only had him for short time I miss Wes coming in to see me. I miss the surprise of what he was bringing me for lunch. I sigh and shake my head to rid myself of those thoughts. No one wants to walk in on a blubbering wreck.

My phone rings and I see it is Wes' cell. I drop my phone like it has burnt me. My heart drops and I feel like I'm about to faint. I grab hold of the side and sit down. It doesn't stop ringing, it continues to ring over and over again. I pick it up and answer it.

"He- hello." I whisper.

"Mi hermana." Jesús sighs.

My fear suddenly turns to pure rage.

"What the hell are you doing?!" I screech.

"Please mi hermana, listen to me. I am just ringing to let you know that I am a changed man. I have not killed any of my staff since I saw you. I also wanted to see that you're okay." He states.

"Seriously, can you hear yourself?! You are ringing me on my dead partner's phone, who you killed! Then you proceed to ask me how I am after you shot me and knocked me unconscious!" I fume.

"Well, yes, I can see why that might seem a little strange to some." He agrees.

"Goodbye Jesús. Destroy the phone. I will be changing my number. I meant what I said, do not ever contact me again. You've put me through enough, leave me alone." I sigh.

"No mi hermana, don't hang up. I wanted to

say goodbye properly. You, despite everything I've done, still gave me a chance. For that I will forever be grateful. Goodbye mi hermana." He says before disconnecting.

I drop my phone and sob. I should have killed him. I should have put an end to him. I will forever be haunted by that decision.

The chime above the door rings. Groaning I quickly grab some tissues and wipe my eyes.

I plaster a fake smile on my face to greet the customer. It's Rubble. I frown in confusion.

"Why are you here? Are the Satans keeping tabs on me or something?" I ask.

He frowns and reaches forward and wipes away a stray tear.

"You've been crying." He points out.

I smile and wipe my face with my hands.

"Yeah I'm fine, just a bit emotional." I shrug, lying.

"What can I get you? The same as Mammoth, an apology bouquet?" I ask.

He shakes his head and holds up a bag.

"Lunch. I know Wes used to stop by with some lunch for you and I figured you would probably miss it. I also wanted to make sure you're eating okay." He states, unloading the tubs of food onto the counter.

I smile and let out a little sob. He head snaps up to look at me.

"Shit, I made you cry." He states.

I wave my hand and try and speak but the tears are falling heavy now. Rubble surprises me and walks around the counter and pulls me into his arms. His hand strokes slowly up and down my back, soothingly.

"I am sorry I cried on you." I state, my cheek resting on his chest. I don't want to let go yet, his arms feel too good, too comforting.

"It's nothing." He states.

"Jesús rang just before you arrived." I say and feel Rubble's body tense.

"It's okay, he rang off of Wes's phone. I guess it must have been in the truck. It threw me a little. He didn't say anything, just goodbye. Still, I think I will be changing my number. I should have killed him when I had the chance." I mumble.

Rubble doesn't say anything, he just holds me for as long as I need him to. I pull away and look up at him and smile.

"Thank you. I needed that."

He nods.

"No problem. Let's eat, I'm starving."

We eat together and it's nice, it's comforting. I tell him about Mammoth's flower purchase and also make him promise not to bust his balls over it.

We finish eating and he has to leave.

"Thanks for this, I needed it." I sigh.

He gives me the cool guy chin lift and leaves.

I found out that day that when you go back to work after a bereavement and you're a part of the Satan's Outlaws, they like to check up on you a lot. For the next week I was lucky enough to get two visitors every day. Rubble brought me lunch and the rest of the family seemed to take it turns. Wes was right, they may be loud, scary, and slightly crazy, but they certainly look after their loved ones.

****

It's Carter and Daisy's wedding reception and I'm sitting in front of my mirror applying my make-up. It's the first time since losing Wes that I've actually made the effort to wear make-up. I'm keeping it simple with the exception of my thick winged eyeliner.

I slip on my black spaghetti strap midi dress; it scoops loosely over my bust while hugging the rest of my curves and my very slight bump. I leave my neck plain and just wear my silver bracelets and bangles. I open my wardrobe and take out my one and only pair of Christian

Louboutin's red soled stiletto shoes. I saved my ass off for this one pair. I only ever wear them on special occasions and with me now being pregnant I'm not sure when I will be able to wear them again.

Running my fingers through my hair I decide to leave it in its natural wavy state. I grab my red clutch bag and my red shawl and head downstairs. I was told someone would be by at six to pick me up.

I check that I have money and my keys and spritz a little perfume on just as the doorbell rings.

I open the door and Khan is waiting. His eyes do a sweep and they alight.

"Holy fuck you look hot." He compliments bluntly.

"Uh, thanks." I mutter.

I shut the door and lock up. Khan holds his hand out.

"After you m'lady." He winks.

I roll my eyes and walk down the drive to his truck.

"Don't hit me for this, but your ass is a thing of beauty. With them heels and that dress, Christ." He groans.

"Khan, while I appreciate your compliments, don't objectify my body or any women's body for that matter. A simple you look nice will do next time." I say, patting his cheek.

We get in the truck and he starts it up and shakes his head.

"Nope, nice wouldn't cut it. You look better than nice. Nice is a bland and boring word, and that is not how you look in that dress." He states before driving off.

I laugh at his unfiltered nature. That is probably the best way to describe him: unfiltered.

We park up at the venue and Khan holds his hand out to help me out of the truck. We walk inside and I feel a few of the brothers glance my way. Lily and Rose call me over. I walk to them and they wolf whistle at me.

"Oh my god! Seriously, you look unbelievable! I mean incredible, and those shoes!" Lily gushes.

I laugh.

"I could say the same for both of you, you guys look stunning." I compliment.

They really do. Lily has a figure hugging deep red wrap dress on that shows off her curves. Rose has on a navy bodycon dress that has a deep lace v-neck.

Patty walks over and looks stunning. She is wearing an emerald green figure hugging dress with a sweetheart neckline and double straps. The green makes her eyes pop.

"Um ladies, to say you're causing a little bit of a stir is an understatement." Raven walks over and whispers to us.

We all turn around and see Rip, Blake, Khan, Axel, Rubble, Mammoth, and practically the rest of the club stood at the bar. All eyes are on us.

"Wow." Patty mutters.

"Yeah. Rip, Axel, and Blake all look like they are about to kill someone." I point out.

Rose snorts.

"Yeah, they get a little possessive. They bang their chests, go all alpha male, that sort of thing. I'm certain Wes would have been exactly the same." She states.

I nod and give her a tight smile. She gasps.

"Oh honey I'm sorry, I didn't mean to bring him up tonight. I'm an ass, just ignore me." She apologises.

"It's fine, honestly. I mean I'm going to have to get used to it right? You guys can't avoid talking about him forever. It's all part of the healing process, well, that's what they say." I smile and shrug.

Lily squeezes my arm and gives me a sad smile. I hate that I want to know when I will be past that point, past the point of pity smiles, pity looks.

"Ladies and gentlemen, please give a big cheer for the bride and groom!" The DJ announces over the mic. We turn around and watch as Daisy and Carter walk in. Everyone cheers and throws confetti at them. They look so happy and Daisy looks so beautiful. Her dress is a long flowing vintage looking dress in a champagne colour with a lace overlay and pearl detailing.

It suddenly all gets too much for me, seeing this amount of love and knowing I won't get that. I step back and slink out of the side door for air, not wanting to disrupt or cause a scene. I don't want to ruin the happy couple's celebration.

I take a deep breath and close my eyes, willing my emotions away.

"It's hard to stomach, seeing other people happy, isn't it." A deep voice sighs.

My eyes snap open and I see Mammoth sitting down on the floor with a bottle of beer in his hands. He looks really unhappy.

I sit down next to him and he offers me a sip of his beer. I shake my head.

"Why are you finding it so hard to watch Daisy and Carter's happiness?" I ask.

He huffs.

"I think it's time for my happiness too but I may have well and truly fucked that up years ago." He takes a pull of his beer. "It's only right, I don't deserve to be happy, not with her anyway."

I frown.

"The girl you brought the flowers for?" I ask.

"Yeah." He sighs.

"I'm going to be brutally honest now, I have never seen you like this and I think if I was to ask the others they would say the same. If she is so important to you, keep what was in the past in the past and don't give up. Don't mope and hide, being too scared for her to say no again, because I'm sure she won't. You like her?" I ask.

"I fuckin' love her." He says honestly.

"Then why the hell are you sat here on the floor moping? You should be planning and thinking of ways you can get her back. If you don't and something changes or something happens, you'll regret it for the rest of your life. So don't be a fuckin whiney moron and miss your chance!" I chastise.

He looks at me. His green eyes start to sparkle and his lips twitch, fighting a smile.

"You giving me some kind of ass whooping pep talk, huh?"

"Yes, yes I am. I lost mine and I'm never

getting him back. Yours is right there, all you have to do is work your ass off to get it. Whatever you did, fix it. Don't stop trying to fix it and when you finally break through with her, you can thank me with chocolate." I smile.

Mammoth puts his arm around me and kisses the top of my head.

"You'll find yours again, it will just take time." He states.

"Maybe, but it will never be him." I sigh.

"There was no one like him, never will be. He was one of a kind." He says, holding his beer up in the air.

"To Wes." He toasts before taking a sip.

CHAPTER THIRTY-THREE

Rip

We watch and celebrate as Carter and Daisy finally get the celebration they deserve.

"Got a minute?" Rubble nods to the door. I nod following him outside.

"What is it?" I ask.

"Jesús contacted Serena." He informs me.

"Why the fuck am I just hearing about this now?" I growl.

"She played it down, said it was nothing, said that he called to say goodbye. Nothing else. She said she would be changing her number. She was shook up. I'm not happy just sitting on it, what if he tries to contact her again? We can't let him have that kind of free reign and power over her or the Satan's Outlaws." Rubble says. He's agitated.

I watch him. His hands are balled up into fists and his jaw is locked tight. The fucker is stressed the fuck out by this, but why?

"If she's okay I don't see a problem. There's not a lot we can do." I shrug, playing him to see if he snaps.

"Fuck, Pres! You're willing to put her life on the line like that?" He asks.

"Well I think she's safe. Jesús doesn't want her dead. He may come and kidnap her one day if he wants to see his sister but he would never harm her." I point out whilst lighting my cigarette.

"Well that's alright then! Fine, you won't do anything about it, I will. I will not let anyone hurt her. Not again. She's been through enough. I will take care of Jesús myself." He threatens.

I smile.

"There it is, that's the real reason isn't it brother? You got a little thing for her? A crush on her? Fuck, Wes is barely cold and you're jumping right on in there aren't you?!" I goad.

Rubble stands nose to nose with me, pure rage pouring off of him.

"I fuckin' love her alright. I fuckin' love her. I would never disrespect Wes like that, don't ever fuckin' suggest I would!" He spits.

He turns. He punches the wall, splitting his

knuckles.

"I will make a call. I'm owed a favour from someone in Mexico. I can't promise a direct kill but this guy knows his explosives." I offer.

Rubble nods.

"And brother, as for Serena, keep away. She belonged to Wes. Do not cross that line, not ever. Go find some club whore to sink your dick into. Get her out of your system." I advise.

Rubble looks to me, eyebrow raised.

"You manage to get Rose out of your system? Tell me, how did that work for you?" He retorts. "Oh yeah, you fuckin' married her!" He yells.

"Watch it Rubble. Rose wasn't a brother's woman, Serena is. You're wanting to hit on his woman! Why don't you just go and piss all over his fuckin' grave?!" I bite back.

"You think so fuckin' little of me, huh? Wes was a brother to me. Do you know what, fuck you! Fuck you Pres!" Rubble spits and flips me off as he gets on his bike and rides off.

"Fuck." I sigh in frustration.

I pull out my cell and make the call.

"Hola."

"Jesús." Is all I say.

"Sorry. Wrong number." He says before disconnecting.

We're always careful incase the feds are listening. Let's hope that this finally destroys Jesús.

I go off in search of Serena and find her outside.

"Serena, I've just spoken with Rubble. He told me about Jesús. Why didn't you say anything?" I ask.

She shrugs.

"I don't know. I just didn't want make it a bigger deal than what it was. I've changed my number so he can't contact me again. I just want to forget about him and not have him poison anymore of my life." She sighs.

"I get that darlin' but in future you let me know. I can't look out for you if I don't know what's going on." I point out.

"Okay fine, but I'm telling you, there will not be a next time." She states before walking off.

I pinch the bridge of my nose.

"Fuck Wes. I already have my own woman who is an independent pain in my ass and now I've got to watch over yours too. Cheers brother." I state, raising my glass before downing my bourbon, the amber liquid warming my throat.

I walk back inside to find my wife. I spot her dancing on the dance floor, swaying her hips and that perfect ass of hers. I walk straight towards her and take her hand, leading her off of the dance floor.

"Rip! What the hell are you doing?" She screeches, practically running to keep up with me.

I turn and give her a look, it's a look she knows well.

"Oh." She whispers as her eyes alight with heat and a sexy smile plays on her lips.

I open a door and find a cleaning closet. I shut us both in there away from the party. She may be a pain in my ass but she always helps to take the stress away.

CHAPTER THIRTY-FOUR

Serena

I fall into a routine of going to work and coming home and sleeping. That's all I do. It keeps me going, the keeping busy, gives me less time to think. It gives me less time to remember that I am lonely.

It's been four months since I lost Wes but it's only in the past month that I have felt lonely. When I went for my scan they told me that I'm having a baby girl. I was elated until it hit me; I have no one to share the excitement with. When I woke up in the middle of the night feeling her kick for the first time, there was no one I could share it with.

The baby shopping, the decorating the nursery, it's just me. Don't get me wrong, the Satan's Outlaws and the girls have been great, but they can't be with me for every milestone. It's just the realisation that this will be my life from here on out, just me and the baby.

As soon as I found out I was having a girl I knew immediately that I wanted to name her after my mother Viola. Well, I had actually decided on Viola Wesley DeRosa. I know it's an unusual thing to name your daughter after their father, but it felt like the right thing to do, an important thing to do.

I pull up into the department store with a huge list of baby items that I need. I've even upgraded my car to a minivan because it's safer and there's more space for the baby and pram.

I get out and grab a flat bed cart. I need a cot, a swinging seat thing that apparently means you're a bad parent if you don't have one, plus a changing bag and so many smaller items.

I find the swinging chair and just about manage to lift it onto the cart. I grab everything else, leaving the cot until last. I grab the box and try to lift it onto the cart but it's too heavy. I heave and squat whilst trying to lift the box on. Not one person stops to help.

"No, no, I'm fine. You just walk on by and leave a pregnant woman to struggle. Selfish assholes!" I yell.

"You know if you need help that's really not the way you go about asking someone." A voice says behind me. It makes me jump.

I spin around and see Rubble leaning on his cart. There's a smile playing on his lips.

"Holy shit! Do not creep up on a pregnant woman." I breathe.

"Sorry. Do you want a hand with that?" He asks.

"That would be amazing thank you." I smile. "See! This is a gentleman right here helping out a pregnant lady!" I yell and point at Rubble.

Rubble grunts and shakes his head. I go to push the cart but Rubble takes it off of me and pushes mine while pulling his behind him.

"At least let me push yours." I offer.

He just ignores me and heads to the checkout. When everything is scanned I go to hand over my card but he stands in the way and gives the cashier his card.

"What the hell do you think you're doing?" I ask stunned.

"Not me, the club. It's the club credit card." He states.

I stand here opening and closing my mouth like a stunned fish.

"But?"

"But nothing. It's the clubs way of looking after their family." He states. "Now come on, I will follow you home and help you to unpack all of this."

He nods for me to lead the way. I walk back to my car, a little dazed from the extravagant gesture.

"You've got to be shitting me? A minivan?" Rubble asks in disbelief.

"Yeah. The dealership said it's safe and practical for an expanding family. All of the parents have one." I state.

"Condoms are safe and practical, but ribbed or flavoured ones are more fun yet still offer the same protection, just like an SUV." He jokes.

I laugh and shake my head. He loads everything into the trunk for me and follows me home.

Once we're back at the house he carries the cot and baby stuff and puts everything in the nursery.

He looks around the room which I decorated myself. I decided on pastel colours. I wanted her room to be soft and feminine but not overly girly.

I had a canvas printed of Wes and placed it up on the wall so she would be able to see her father's face. It's my favourite picture of him because he's laughing.

I catch Rubble staring at his picture and smile.

"I took that on my phone when we were play fighting. I thought it would be nice for her to see him every day." I explain.

"It's a good idea." He answers.

"Can I get you a coffee or a tea? Both decaf of course. I'm afraid I don't have any beers. I haven't bought alcohol in what feels like forever." I offer.

"Um, just a water would be great thanks." He nods.

We head into the kitchen and I put the kettle on and grab him a bottle of water from the fridge.

I make myself a cup of herbal tea, something I would have gagged at before but now apparently I can't get enough of it.

I sip my tea and smile. Rubble looks uncomfortable and there's an awkward silence.

"I should get going. Don't go shopping for heavy items like that on your own again. Next time call me." He says.

"Sure. I need to be getting on with putting this cot together. I think I'm good, all of the large items are done now. Thanks though." I smile.

"You're building the cot now?" He asks.

"Err, yeah, I hate doing half a job. The room is decorated so now I want it done." I shrug.

"Where are your tools?" He asks.

"Under the stairs. Why? I am quite capable of building the cot by myself." I yell after him as he walks off.

I follow him upstairs and watch as he starts unpacking the cot pieces.

"Did you hear what I said? I am more than capable of building the cot myself." I repeat.

"Yeah I heard. Pass me the allen key would you?" He asks.

I look in my toolbox and stare blankly.

"What the hell is an allen key?"

He looks up at me and rolls his eyes. He reaches for pipe looking thing with ridges on it.

"Well if you had just said the pipey thing with ridges on I would have known what you meant." I defend.

He ignores me and continues to build the cot.

"Well if you insist on doing this I'm going to sit and read." I huff.

I sit on the couch with my legs up and start reading. It's not long before I feel my eyes become heavy and fall asleep.

"Serena." My name is whispered.

"Serena. Wake up." Is whispered again.

I moan, still half asleep. I feel warm lips touch mine and I kiss them back. I love the feel of soft lips caressing mine. The kiss deepens and I moan. The soft lips kiss along my neck.

"Wes." I breathe.

Suddenly everything stops. My eyes flutter open in confusion. It takes a moment to fully wake up. I see Rubble next to me, leaning over, hurt across his face. It dawns on me.

"Oh Rubble…I…oh I'm so sorry." I whisper.

He strokes my face, leans forward, and kisses my forehead softly.

"Goodbye Serena, I'm sorry." He says before getting up and leaving.

"Rubble wait…I…" I shout but the door slams shut.

I sit up and put my head in my hands. A few stray tears fall out of guilt to Wes and to Rubble. I was in such a deep sleep that I thought I was kissing Wes.

I walk upstairs, deciding to go to bed. I pause as the nursery catches my eye. I step into the room and look around. Rubble has built the cot and put all of the bedding I have in it. He has also set up the swinging chair. He even hung up the curtains. I place my hand on my heart. The room is perfect. He did all of this while I slept downstairs.

I sob, feeling even more awful. I spot a pink bunny placed on the cabinet and smile; Rubble must have bought it. I pick it up and bring it with me when I climb into bed.

The next morning I drive over to the clubhouse and go in search of Rubble.

"Hey Mammoth, have you seen Rubble?" I ask.

"Well look at you! Shit! Pregnant and still just as beautiful." He winks.

"Thanks, but, um, Rubble?" I ask.

"Packing up his stuff in his room." Mammoth nods.

"Why? Where is he going?" I ask.

"He is off to the Louisiana Chapter. They've made a bit of a mess so he has volunteered to go and sort it out." He States.

I don't respond. I walk to Rubble's room. I don't knock, I just walk straight in. His head snaps up as I enter.

"You're leaving." I state.

He nods.

"Yeah. I figured I would volunteer as the other guys have commitments and loved ones. I don't have anything keeping me here, do I?" He says as he turns to me.

"I…I…" I try to say the words.

He walks to me and cups my face, running his thumb across my bottom lip. He smiles sadly.

"It's okay. I was wrong to kiss you. I was wrong to fall in love with another brother's woman. I don't expect you to ever return my feelings but I can't stay and not have you, it hurts too much." He says before kissing my forehead and zipping up his bag.

"I'm so sorry Rubble, I really am. I wish I could feel the same, I do, because then I wouldn't be in pain or lonely anymore. But I still love Wes so much." I sob.

"It's okay, you don't need to apologise." He sighs. "Look after yourself and the baby." He says as he walks past me, leaving me standing in his room.

I sit on his bed just letting the tears fall. Mammoth sticks his head in and frowns.

"Why are you sitting in here crying?" He asks and sits next to me.

"It's just all one big mess. Why can't I be over Wes already? I am tired of hurting and I am tired of being alone. I am scared of having this baby on my own." I sob.

Mammoth pulls me into his side and rubs my shoulder.

"You will get there one day at a time darlin', I promise. You ever feel like you're alone, ring me. I will come round and talk to you until you're sick of the sight of me. You'll be begging to be alone again." He jokes.

I laugh.

"I doubt that. You have your lady, you can't be keeping me company all the time."

"Yeah well, I haven't broken through that barrier yet. At this rate I don't think I will. So it looks like you're stuck with me." He shrugs.

I wipe my tears and smile up at Mammoth.

"Don't give up." I say, patting his leg and standing.

"Don't plan on it." He winks.

I walk out to my car and see Rubble get on his bike. I stand and watch him ride off.

I wish life could be simpler but if it were, I would never have had my time with Wes. He walked in my life, made me smile, made me laugh. He stole my heart and soul completely even if it was just for a short time. I wouldn't change anything because having a short time with Wes is worth more to me than never having had him in my life at all. I will raise our daughter and tell her about her father every day. I will tell her exactly how the strongest and most powerful love was built. Our love was built on hidden truths.

THE END

EPILOGUE

Serena

I lock up the store early because I'm not feeling right. My back is throbbing and I cannot seem to ease it or get comfy. Climbing into my car I start driving home. Not five minutes into the journey I feel wet between my legs.

"Oh fuck, please not now." I moan.

Pain starts moving all around from my back to my front.

"Oh god that hurts." I breathe.

My due date isn't for another two weeks but clearly she is ready to come out now. I don't have long before another contraction hits. It's stronger this time. It makes me curl forward and grip my steering wheel tight and in doing so I swerve the car, nearly causing an accident.

"Shit." I cry out.

They don't ease up, they only get worse. I

swerve and pull up on the side of the road, unable to continue to drive. I try reaching for my phone but it's in the back seat and I can't quite reach it.

"Damn it!" I cry.

I practically fall out of the car and waddle to the back passenger door. I try to reach for my phone but another contraction hits. I clutch my stomach and try to breathe through it.

I hear shouting across the street. I look up and see Mammoth and a woman arguing.

"Just leave me alone Mammoth!" She yells back at him.

"Riley, just fucking hear me out." He begs back.

I don't really care at this point who Riley is, I need Mammoth. I shout.

"Mammoth!" I yell. He looks up and squints. "Mammoth, aaahhh shit. Help!" I yell.

To my surprise the woman shakes her head and runs across the road to me.

"Hey, are you alright?" She asks.

I grip hold of her hand.

"In labour. I'm in pain, so much pain!" I cry.

"Okay, come on. Get in the back seat, Mammoth will drive you." She states.

"Shit Serena, get in the back. Riley, you sit

in the back with her in case something happens." He orders.

She starts to argue but I grip her hand as another contraction hits.

"Breathe. Breathe." She tries to coach.

"Thanks." I pant.

I look up and her and realise who she is.

"Riley." I sigh and she nods and smiles. "Riley from the restaurant."

Her face suddenly realises.

"Oh yes! It's you! You were with Wes." She smiles.

"Mammoth, you should call him." Riley states to Mammoth.

"He can't." I pant.

"Riley." Mammoth calls.

She ignores him and carries on.

"Oh gosh I'm sorry! Is it not his? Did it not work out for you?" She asks.

"Riley." He calls her name again but she just ignores him.

"He died." I groan.

The car goes silent.

"Um…shit." She splutters. "A heads up would have been good." She chastises Mammoth.

"I fuckin' tried woman but as usual you didn't let me get a word in." He complains.

"Don't start now." She fires back.

"I'm not fuckin' starting." He sighs.

"Uhh guys." I cry but they just ignore me and continue to argue.

"You are! Just because I won't listen to your excuses you accuse me of not listening!" She snaps.

"Guys." I moan.

"You don't ever listen, you only hear what you want to hear." He shouts.

Mammoth swerves the car, causing other cars to beep.

"Fuck you!" Mammoth yells out of the window.

"Go careful, Mammoth. There's a pregnant woman in the back here having a baby." She tuts.

"Guys." I whimper.

"Don't go busting my balls…"

"GUYS!" I scream. They both immediately stop their argument.

"I need to push, I can feel something." I pant.

"Oh fuck." Mammoth sighs. He pulls over and turns to face the back.

"You need to check." He says to Riley.

"Why me? How the hell do I know what to look for?"

"Well a fuckin' baby would be a good start." Mammoth says and rolls his eyes.

"One of you just look! Mammoth, call a fuckin' ambulance!" I yell.

"Okay." Riley says, rubbing her hands together like she is warming them up.

"Why are you warming up your hands? You're just looking! You're not giving me an examination!" I pant.

"Right, I know that, I just…it doesn't matter." She mumbles.

She lifts up my skirt and has a look.

"Um, can you remove your panties?" She asks awkwardly.

I lift my bottom up and pull them down. She takes a deep breath and looks.

"Oh my god. Oh my god." She panics.

"What?!" I ask scared.

"Definitely a baby. It's head…it's…um… right there." She gestures.

"Fuck." Mammoth blurts. "The EMTs are on their way."

"Oh god I need to push." I moan.

"Right then, just push." Riley says.

"What?" Mammoth and I both ask.

"Do what your body is telling you. Mammoth, take off your kutte." She orders.

"What? Why?" He asks.

"For the baby!" She orders and holds out her hand.

He hands her his kutte and I get the urge to push so I do. I scream and push with everything I have.

"That's it! The head is coming out." Riley encourages.

I stop and pant.

"Oh god it hurts." I cry.

"It will but the head is there. Come on! Don't give up! Keep going for a little while longer and baby will be here." She reassures.

I feel another contraction so I push and push. I scream through the pain. I flop down, exhausted. Little cries fill the car. I open my eyes and see Riley smiling wide, holding my baby wrapped in a Satan's Outlaws kutte.

"Well fuck me." Mammoth mutters.

Riley lays her on me. I look down and I am immediately in love. Her little scrunched up face staring back at me.

"Hey Viola. I'm your mommy." I sigh.

The car is silent. In the distance we can hear the sirens of the EMTs on their way. I look up at Riley who is looking lovingly at Mammoth. He is looking at her the same way. I smile.

"Thank you, both of you." I rasp with emotion.

Moment broken they both turn to me and smile.

"Viola Wesley DeRosa. I will always be here for you for every day of your life. Your Daddy will watch over you too, protecting you from heaven." I sniff, wiping away my tears.

My heart has been empty for so long since losing Wes but now it is filled with love for my baby daughter. I will never be alone and she will never be alone. We will always have each other and Wes' love and protection from above.

The EMTs put me onto a stretcher. As they wheel me onto the ambulance a white feather flutters down from the sky and lands on my legs. He will always be with me, always protecting me.

THANK YOU FOR READING HIDDEN TRUTHS, BOOK ONE IN THE SATAN'S OUTLAWS SERIES.

Book two of the Satan's Outlaws series will be coming in Spring 2021.

If you would like to get to know Lily, Daisy, Rose, and Axel, their stories are told in The Rocke series which is available on Amazon and free on Kindle Unlimited.

Also available on Amazon and Kindle Unlimited is Tiers of Joy, a standalone romantic comedy.

For all upcoming releases, teasers, and giveaways, follow me on social media, Goodreads, and Bookbub.

Printed in Great Britain
by Amazon